Witch Hunt

by

Sara Bourgeois

Chapter 1

The morning sunlight streamed across the lobby of
the Dimidio Inn. It caught on the old, but well-kept armchairs
and spread across the antique rug. Behind the front desk,
Reva Brennan adjusted a vase of peonies to face out into the
lobby and pulled out the guest book. She set it on the counter
and used her magic to set the spoon in her coffee cup spinning.
The milk in her cup swirled until the whole drink was the
same gentle tan. Satisfied, Reva took a drink and sighed
happily.

It was a beautiful morning, there were guests in her
family's inn, and she had a fresh cup of coffee. Life couldn't
get much better.

Cyrus Hawthorne got up silently from his seat in the
corner, crossed the room, and leaned his arms on the front
desk.

"Can I get a room for the night?"

Reva rolled her eyes, but humored him by opening up
the book. She tucked a lock of her red hair behind her ear as

she scanned her openings. In reality, there were two rooms, but instead she said,

"I'm so sorry, I think we're all full. You're going to have to rough it at the cemetery down the street."

"You don't say." Cyrus raised his eyebrows. He smoothed his moustache. "Sounds like you're quite successful at this innkeeping business."

Reva grinned.

"Not too bad, if I do say so myself."

Even though she was being sarcastic, she still felt a gentle glow of pride when she looked around and remembered everything she had accomplished at the Dimidio Inn.

"I have always appreciated a young lady who knows her own value," Cyrus said.

"Wow," Reva said sarcastically. "You're pretty modern for someone who's been dead for over a hundred years."

"Why thank you," Cyrus said, brushing ghostly dust off his velvet overcoat and adjusting his cravat. "I do try to keep up."

"You must have very good influences."

"Oh I do," Cyrus agreed. "One Miss Brennan. Perhaps you've met her."

"Nope," Reva shook her head. "Never heard of her, sounds suspicious."

Cyrus's brows knit together.

"I don't find you suspicious at all," he said. "You run a hotel full of ghosts. Utterly normal."

"I agree," Reva said. "As long as the rest of the living people don't find out."

"You leave a few rooms for them," Cyrus said flippantly, pointing in the guest book to the three rooms that they'd set aside for mortals. "They're fine."

"I guess we've got it all figured out," Reva agreed.

"A perfect partnership."

She finished her coffee and sighed happily. Cyrus had been helping her run the Dimidio Inn since her parents had died. Most days, she didn't know what she'd do without him.

Reva had been nervous taking over her family's business by herself. There had been a lot to learn and she'd made some mistakes here and there, but she'd always kept her head above water. It helped to have such a devoted friend in Cyrus.

They'd met when she'd first arrived at the Inn. She'd been surprised to learn that Cyrus was actually happier as a ghost, but when Reva learned about the tragedies of his mortal life, she didn't blame him at all.

"What are you doing this afternoon?" he asked. "May I have the honor of taking you to tea?"

3

"Can't," Reva told him. "I need to catch up with my Aunt Alva."

Cyrus's face fell, his moustache drooping sadly, but after a moment, he brightened.

"What about tomorrow afternoon?"

"Okay," Reva said hesitantly. "But what about your ghost gossip sessions in the cemetery? You haven't been over there all week."

It was unusual that a ghost like Cyrus spent so much time away from the cemetery that sat alongside the Inn. But whenever Reva asked him about it, he always had a similar response.

"I do enjoy spending time with the other denizens of the Yews," Cyrus admitted. "They do have infinitely better gossip than you mortals, but I prefer to occupy myself here. There's so much to do."

"Yup," Reva said absently. She turned back to the guest book, making note of who was checking out that day and who would need fresh linens (only mortals, of course). Satisfied, she closed the book and grinned at Cyrus.

"You spend most, if not all of your time, by my side anyways. What if we don't have anything to talk about at tea?"

4

"Impossible!" Cyrus levitated slightly off the ground, prepared to defend himself, but he was interrupted by a ball of fluff bursting through the door.

Pistol the kitten darted into the lobby, tumbling over the welcome mat and skidding to a stop on the carpet. He had clearly just been out in the dusty parking lot. His grey tabby fur was coated in dust and he had left tiny kitten paw prints on the rustic floorboards.

"Hey," Cyrus scolded Pistol. "Watch where you're putting those dirty paws of yours. We're trying to run a respectable establishment here."

"Never mind that," Pistol cut him off. The kitten shook more of the dust out of his fur and launched himself up on to the front desk. He pawed at the guest book.

"Do you have any vacancies? Looks like we might have a new guest."

"Really?" Reva whipped the book back open. Cyrus came around the desk to peer over her shoulder. "I've got options, but it depends on how long they want to stay. Just one person, not a couple or a family?"

Reva hadn't been joking when she told Cyrus that business was good, but it wouldn't hurt to have another mortal customer to keep up appearances.

"Just one cool character in a leather jacket," Pistol said. "I saw him out in the parking lot. Tall, bearded, very

5

serious. Not only wearing a leather jacket, but fancy pants shoes too. He definitely means business."

"Then I guess it depends what his business is," Reva said thoughtfully. "Are you sure he's looking for a room?"

"Well, I definitely haven't seen him around Shadow Woods before," Pistol said. "I would remember those shoes."

Out of the corner of her eye, Reva saw Cyrus roll his eyes and sniff haughtily. She sighed under her breath. The ghosts were always suspicious of newcomers. She was about to remind him that a fresh face was not the end of the world, when the front door opened.

The man was just as Pistol had described him. Tall, serious, and very well-dressed. But Pistol had failed to mention that the man was good looking as well. The man pulled off his sunglasses and nodded to Reva.

"This your hotel?" he asked.

"Yes," Reva said brightly, ignoring Cyrus's glare. "Welcome to the Dimidio Inn, serving the community of Shadow Woods for generations."

"Nice place."

Cyrus made another grumbling noise and began to tap his finger loudly on the book he had been reading all morning.

"Would you like a room?" Reva asked over the noise. For all that Cyrus was helpful, she wished he would leave the mortal guests alone. Especially the mortal men. Thank heaven this newcomer didn't appear to see him, but he could likely hear him.

"Definitely not," the man said brusquely.

All three beings behind the counter stiffened at his tone. Cyrus tapped his book even louder. The man pulled out a black leather wallet and flipped it open to reveal a shining gold detective's badge.

"Detective Matt Carver," he said. "There's been a murder in the cemetery next to your property."

All three beings behind the counter stiffened again for entirely different reasons.

"Someone's been murdered?" Reva gasped.

"It's common courtesy to let you know that there's been an incident," Matt said as if Reva hadn't said anything. "You might see us in the neighborhood, but we ask that you mind your own business."

Reva opened her mouth, but Matt cut her off.

"What's that noise?"

Cyrus froze.

"What noise?" Reva asked innocently.

"It's like a strange tapping noise," Matt said.

Next to Reva, Cyrus experimentally tapped three more times on his book.

"That!" Matt explained.

"Oh, that." Reva laughed loudly. She tried to kick Cyrus discretely and stumbled.

"Are you okay?" Matt asked.

"I'm fine," Reva said quickly. "It's nothing. Just some old pipes that I really should get checked, but you know, it's an old building, what are you going to do?"

Detective Carver didn't look convinced. That was exactly what Reva needed. Some grumpy, obnoxiously handsome, stranger sticking his nose in her business. On the other hand, Cyrus's face was gleeful as he realized he could mess with said grumpy mortal who couldn't see him at all.

And even worse, there had just been a murder in her cemetery.

Chapter 2

Glaring at her with narrowed eyes, Matt frowned deeply before taking a glance around at the inn's lobby. Reva didn't appreciate the way this newcomer came into her cherished establishment and started stink-eyeing the place. Based on the way Cyrus and Pistol mirrored her distaste, she knew she wasn't alone with that sentiment.

His sour attitude shadowed the true issue at hand. A murder in *The Yews*... Reva and Auntie Alva worked diligently to uphold the good reputation of the cemetery. After all, the public graveyard harbored an unfathomable amount of town history. To hear that someone was murdered in the very place where the dead were supposed to find peace was troubling, to say the least.

"What's up with that cat?" Matt nodded towards Pistol. The familiar responded with a low hiss, arching his back into a c-shape and unsheathing his tiny claws. "Weird."

"So you're coming into my hotel and insulting my kitten?" Reva asked, leaning against the counter with one arm. "You've got lots of nerve, Mister."

"If I didn't have nerve, I wouldn't be in the position I am right now."

"You're new," Reva said, staring at the designer shoes that Pistol mentioned when he first charged in. Shadow Woods didn't have designer stores. Those establishments didn't exist for miles around. "Definitely not a local."

"Good observational skills. I'm sure anyone with two eyes and a functioning brain could have figured that one out."

Cyrus scoffed, standing firmly beside Reva. He leaned in, voice low.

"Reva, forgive me for interrupting, since you and I *both* know that you can handle yourself excellently, but would you like me to help in leading this…" Cyrus eyed him and held back a gag. "…*gentleman* to the exit?"

With a slight shake of the head, Reva continued her conversation with the detective. Due to the potent animosity in the air, their ambience felt more suited for a gunfight.

"Why did you come to Shadow Woods in the first place? Surely, someone like you didn't leave behind luxuries and glamor for a tiny town like ours for no reason, right?"

"Why would you assume that I *lived* with luxury and glamor?" Matt chuckled, crossing his arms tightly. "Not even close."

"That doesn't answer my original question."

"I came to this town because your police department needed all the help they could get on their force. Apparently, this precinct didn't even have a lead detective to tackle cases," he explained, a flare of pride lining his words. "I was happy to accept the position and help fill a much-needed leadership role."

"Who does this guy think he is?" Pistol growled, making a gradual round through the lobby to stare at the detective from all directions. "Big deal. He took a job that someone else in town was bound to fill up eventually. He's got a fat head."

Again, Reva thanked the stars for the detective's ignorance. He clearly didn't speak cat, so Pistol's words would sound like innocuous yips and yowls.

"As well as an exceptionally obtuse demeanor, if I may add. I'm still wondering whether he's being deliberate with his word choice or if his dullness is a natural part of his personality," Cyrus quipped. "It's clear he's too arrogant for his own good."

"And now…" Reva wiped away the dust on her countertop. "You've got your first big-boy case. That's great to hear."

"Someone got *murdered* on the property next door and this is how you respond?"

"Tell me more about the murder, then, and let's stop dancing around the details," Reva shot back, earning her a scowl. "What happened? Was it particularly violent? I don't want any potential customers to get scared away by something like this."

Chuckling under his breath, Matt took a moment to compose himself. He wiped at his nose, sending Reva a half-smile that did nothing but spark more contempt in her heart for him. So new, yet the detective managed to push nearly all of her buttons on the first try. Impressive.

"I did some light reading on your hotel before coming here. You've got a pretty remarkable place, I'll give you that."

Her hands balled up into fists.

"However, I saw that you don't get a lot of customers around here," he said. Jutting his thumb over his shoulder, he continued. "Murder or not, people don't tend to stay at this hotel. I wonder why that's the case."

"Is there a reason why you're asking me these questions, detective? Or am I going to have to knock myself out trying to crack that one?"

"Funny," he deadpanned. "I was just asking a simple question."

"I want to bite him," Pistol admitted, hopping off the counter, lowering himself against the ground, and wiggling his body. "There's not much he can do if I go for his ankles now. I'll scratch up those thousand-dollar sneakers of his, while I'm at it."

"I don't recommend that, my beloved cat," Cyrus replied.

"Why not?" Pistol's ears twitched. "What will he do? Fling me against the wall? I'll get him hit with a felony charge if he tries it."

"I suggest that we work on getting him off the property, instead." Taking a glimpse at Reva, he smiled. "She'll figure something out, I'm sure."

"Uh-huh." The familiar rolled his eyes. "If it were me in her shoes, he would have already been tossed off the property, just saying."

"I can't answer your questions. In fact, I don't even want to," she admitted with a shrug. "I haven't committed a crime. I don't even bother anyone, for that matter, so I don't understand why you're coming at me like I'm a suspect."

"Slow down." Matt held up a hand. "No one is coming at you. I just wanted to let you know about what happened. The fact that our conversation took this route isn't something I anticipated."

"And yet you helped nudge it down that path regardless," she countered. "Just tell me about the victim. Who was it?"

Bracing herself, she hoped that it wasn't a close friend of hers. She had enough on her plate to deal with and she didn't need to hear about a dear friend getting killed near her property.

"His name was Burton Crabb." Matt gauged her reaction. "Do you know him?"

"Of course I do," she answered, rather curtly. "Shadow Woods isn't that big of a town, you know. Everyone knows everyone."

"Thanks for that tidbit of knowledge, I'll tuck it away for later," he said, sarcastically. "I already knew that, just so you know."

"Really? I thought you were new and clueless."

"The victim owned a local ghost tour service in town called *Terror Tales*. Apparently, one of the tour features was walking through distinguished... and 'haunted' places in Shadow Woods." Matt placed air quotes around the word. "Sounds like a waste of money, but I'm not one to judge."

"Ironic," she whispered, intended for Cyrus. "The only thing he's done since he's got here is judge."

"Do you have any useful information that might help push this investigation forward?" Matt asked, reaching into his jacket and pulling out a notepad. In one of his pockets, he retrieved a pen. "Anything helps."

"I want to see the crime scene."

"I'm afraid I can't let you do that."

"Why not?" Reva rounded the corner, already headed towards the hotel's entrance. "I take care of that cemetery with my aunt. I want to see what happened."

Sighing deeply, Matt's arms dropped limply at his sides.

"You shouldn't stick your nose in police business. Right now, the cemetery is closed off since the body is still there. I have officers in there collecting prints, taking photos, and finding evidence. You can't just saunter into the scene."

"That cemetery means a lot to me," she maintained, swatting his hand away once he tried to reach out and stop her from passing him. "Whatever happens in there *is* my business.

14

I don't need someone like you trying to keep me out of a place that I consider part of my home."

"What?" Matt sent her a bewildered gaze. "That's a public graveyard. I have never heard someone say that a *graveyard* is like their home."

Mortals will never understand, she thought hopelessly to herself. *The Yews is where all my friends are.*

Instead of revealing that detail to him, she managed a fiery "Be quiet" as she pushed her way out the doors and towards the cemetery. Matt stuck close behind, trying to talk her out of going. Behind the counter, Cyrus watched on proudly as Reva shoved the detective back into his place.

Pistol lapped at his paw, cleaning his whiskers.

"It's a good thing he left," the familiar said. "I was about to shred his fancy pants."

Chapter 3

Reva stopped abruptly near the cemetery's front gates, processing the shock in seeing the heavy police presence flooding her beloved graveyard. Camera shutters sounded off as crime scene photographers snapped images of Burton's body that lay across two gravesites. From afar, she could only see his motionless feet that poked out from behind tombstones.

15

"What happened to him?" Reva asked wistfully, staring long at the gravestones positioned neatly across *The Yews*.

Matt's seemingly perpetual frown persisted as Reva tried to push her way into the cemetery against his verbal commands.

"Can you stop that?" Matt snapped. "You're not supposed to be here. If anything, you're impeding the investigation."

"By doing what, exactly? Standing off to the side while I let the police officers do their job?" Reva scoffed, swatting his hand away for the umpteenth time. "Give me a break."

"Civilians aren't–"

"You've said that too many times already, it's getting annoying."

Matt's eyes widened briefly.

"I don't think I'm the annoying one, in all honesty. I've told you that you can't be here and you've decided to go against my orders. I wouldn't have even approached you if I knew you were going to be this irritating about it."

"I would have found out eventually," she informed, turning around to shoot daggers at him from her dark eyes. "It's right next to my property. A crowd of police officers taping the place off and snapping pictures would have been difficult to miss."

Matt probably knew that his current approach in dealing with Reva wasn't going to work. Instead, he closed his eyes and sucked in a few deep breaths. Running his tongue over his teeth, he fought to keep his temper to a manageable level.

"Look. I'm sorry for how things played out up until now, but I really don't need any more problems." He gestured his hand towards Burton's body. "I've got a case to work on and evidence to look over. You don't have any business here, so I'm going to ask you to leave."

The rational side of her tried to put herself in Matt's shoes. A detective who came into a new town, already thrust into a murder investigation. She figured that he didn't have any family in town and he didn't know anyone quite yet, so he didn't have anyone to lean on. To an extent, she could empathize with him.

However, she also acknowledged that the detective hadn't made a positive impression on her. From his tone to his attitude, the dude rivaled vinegar with his bitterness. She couldn't care less about his half-hearted attempt to save the burning bridge between them that was already nearly charred.

"You've got a big mouth for someone who knows nothing about the town or its citizens," she hurled back, each word laced with venom.

Turning away, Reva didn't catch the moment where her words lit a fire under the detective. Jaw clenching hard enough for the veins in his forehead to protrude, Matt couldn't find the words to reply. Stunned by her audacious nature, he didn't even react in time to stop Reva from approaching the police tape, standing on her toes to try and catch a glimpse of the action.

"Hey!" Matt stormed over. "Get away from here! I've had enough of this."

"Shut up already," she whispered, finally seeing the state of Burton's body. "Oh, wow."

With an arrow wedged deeply into his chest, Burton didn't stand a chance against the person who snatched his life away with ease. One tug of the bowstring, followed by the quick and abrupt release of an arrow, and that was all it took to send the poor man to an early grave. Reva closed her eyes, hoping that his spirit could find peace.

"Did you even listen to me?"

"Not really," she admitted. "I have better things to think about."

Suddenly, she felt a large hand clamped over her forearm. A surprised gasp fell from her lips as Matt tugged her away from the crime scene, all the way back to the gated entrance. Protesting loudly, Reva dug her fingernails underneath his hands in an attempt to pry his palm away from her skin. His strength outmatched hers, unfortunately. Obstructing the entrance, Matt crossed his arms over his chest.

"Sorry about that, but you were getting on my last nerve."

"That doesn't give you a right to *touch* me!" Reva exclaimed, rubbing the whitened spot on her arm where he applied the pressure. "There's something seriously wrong with you if you think you can just do that to people."

Rolling his eyes, Matt didn't take her words seriously. Battling against the urge to shoot a spell into his face, Reva averted her gaze and tried to think about the things that made her happy. Small animals, her aunt's cooking, night-time television binges. Anything besides the smug detective that barricaded her view of *The Yews*.

"You didn't give me a choice," he said. "You weren't responding to my verbal requests, so I had to take matters into my own hands."

"I can see that the police force added an *admirable* member to their team," she spat.

"Your jabs might have stung a little while ago, but now that I've seen a good glimpse of your personality, they don't do much to me any more. What?" Matt cocked a brow.

19

"An entitled business owner who thinks she can kick and shove her way to anything she wants? I'm horrified."

"You know *nothing* about me," Reva hissed. "Don't start assuming things about my life."

"I could ask the same of you."

Shaking her head, she realized that she didn't feel like having another petty battle with the detective who just couldn't get a clue. Her eyes skimmed across the tall metal gates that encapsulated the cemetery, noticing small details that appeared out of place.

In particular, she spotted homemade signs a few feet away from the front entrance. Her stomach dropped to the ground, recognizing the handwriting that spelled out the threatening words.

Burton Crabb: Stay out of this cemetery for your own good. Your presence is not wanted here.

Noticing her silence, Matt followed her gaze and noticed the signs, as well. She blinked out of her daze, shaking off the jitters that suddenly overwhelmed her.

"What's that?" Matt asked, nodding towards the signs. "Who put those there?"

"I don't know," she lied. "People put messages on the cemetery gates all the time, it's never that big of a deal."

"Sure, but this sign is addressing the victim that was just found with an arrow clean through his heart," he pointed out, approaching the signs and narrowing his eyes as he scrutinized the message. "Who wanted to keep Burton out of this place?"

"How should I know?" Reva asked.

That was Auntie Alva's writing, clear as day. She could tell because her aunt wrote her m's and w's in a distinctive manner, with round edges instead of sharper ones. Her mind spun, wondering why her aunt wanted to keep Burton out of the cemetery. What animosity did the two share? Her throat went dry and her heart rate picked up as she watched the detective snap photos of the signs with his phone.

"Are you sure you don't know about the person who set these signs here?" Matt asked again, scrolling through the photos he just took. "As you said, you take care of this cemetery. Surely, you would have a good idea about the types of people that frequent this spot."

"I already told you that I don't," she maintained. She shrugged, keeping up a nonchalant act that threatened to crack if Matt pressed her with the right questions. "Could be anyone, really."

Pocketing his phone, the detective glanced at the signs once more before focusing upon her. A dry chuckle followed.

"I don't believe you, sorry to say."

Her cheeks reddened, a result of her silent frustration and anger. She kept her expression blank, as best as she could.

"Lucky for me, there's other ways to identify the person who set those signs there. Who knows? What if you were the one who placed them?"

"That's a stretch," she huffed, shuffling her weight between her feet. "I didn't have an issue with Burton. He was just another business owner trying to make ends meet."

Humming, Matt nodded slowly.

"Sure. I'll figure out the truth sooner or later about what really happened here. For your sake, I really hope you didn't play a role in this entire mess." The slight fragment of a self-satisfied smile fell away from his face. "And if you're covering up for anyone, I'll find out about that, too."

Chapter 4

Staring down at her phone, Reva opened her text message conversation with Aunt Alva. Reading over the message she received nearly two hours ago, Reva almost hid her face in her hands in frustration.

Reva! I'm so sorry to say this, but I won't be able to catch up with you this afternoon. Something else came up, but you can find me at my cottage later today. I love you, dear!

"What trouble did you get yourself into?" she mumbled, fraught with worry. "I can't let that detective mess with you, Auntie. I just can't."

Deciding that it was futile to just sit around and bite her nails all day, Reva decided to make her time useful. To keep her mind off of the impending stress that threatened to cripple her if she thought about it too long, she rolled up her sleeves, snapped on some rubber gloves that shielded her skin up to her elbows, and started cleaning the kitchen.

Taking out her frustrations on the grime and grease that plagued her pots and pans, she scrubbed until she felt her arms ready to come off. For more efficiency, she uttered a spell that caused nearby dishes and utensils to rise into the air, as well as cleaning sponges. The dishwashing solution flew across the kitchen, spurting green upon each sponge. Commanding the bottle back into its place, Reva focused on cleaning seven pots simultaneously with only two hands, her magic taking care of six.

She worked quickly, desperately hoping that her mortal customers didn't accidentally poke their heads through the door and see the eye-popping sight. She didn't want to explain why six sponges cleaned six pots without anyone to guide them.

"I should do this more often," she mused, realizing how fast work went by when she used her magic as a small boost.

Thankfully, worries about the murder in *The Yews* subsided while she cleaned. When she finished, panting as she

23

leaned upon the spotless kitchen island, the thoughts bubbled up after simmering in silence. Her aunt and her involvement kept lingering, anguishing her. Was there a chance…?

No. Reva didn't believe it. Her aunt was a sweet, empathetic witch that wouldn't mind peeling off the clothes from her back to give them to someone else. She didn't know the issues Alva had with Burton, but Reva *knew* that her aunt didn't kill that man. That didn't sit right with her.

Her pensive silence was soon interrupted by boisterous laughter coming from the nearby lobby. Taking off her gloves and setting them to the side, Reva made her way out to see Cyrus chatting it up with another curious ghost that often stopped by *The Dimidio Inn* for some fun and good conversation.

Rory Simmons was aged thirty-five when he died in a boating accident gone wrong off the coast of Maine. He found a pleasant community at *The Yews* and, like many of the spirits that still lingered in the graveyard, liked discussing drama that didn't concern him directly. The scandals of the mortal world knew no bounds. Considering they all owned human bodies at one point, that was a fact these spirits knew well.

Cyrus' eyes lit up when he saw Reva entering the lobby and nudged Rory's arm. The ghost turned around and greeted her with a smile.

"Nice to see you again, Reva!" Rory said. "I was thinking about renting myself a room for a night or two. There's been too much commotion next door and it's really draining my energy, you know? We can't talk too loud with the police around since they might overhear us."

"You're giving them far too much credit, my friend," Cyrus replied. "They probably mistake your voices for the wind."

"Those cops keep complaining that they feel as if our graveyard is creepy. Can you believe it?" Rory smacked his palm on the counter. "One day, they'll probably make their own stops at *The Yews*. If they could only realize the world they're missing out on, I bet they wouldn't look at our graveyard with such fear in their eyes."

"You can't blame them for acting that way," Reva pointed out, rounding the counter to stand beside Cyrus. He beamed, leaning on his hand and staring at her while she spoke. "They don't know any better."

"I guess you have a point," Rory conceded. "It's just annoying to have them poking around in our stuff. I saw them taking signs off of the gate entrance earlier."

Reva realized she hadn't seen any other signs on the cemetery besides the ones Auntie Alva left behind for Burton. She paled. They were taking them in as evidence.

25

"Did they say why they were doing that?" Cyrus asked, taking the words right from Reva's mouth. The fear that pooled in her chest hampered her ability to speak. "I suspect they have a reason."

"They said something about fingerprints and a possible suspect leaving behind a message for the victim to find. All that boring talk that serves no purpose to me," Rory answered, running a hand through his hair. He was a dark blond in life, like Cyrus. "I can't wait until they leave. They're messing up the tranquil environment at *The Yews*."

"Did you see that detective? He walks around as if he owns the bloody place," Cyrus said, punctuated by a disgusted scowl. "He came in here looking for trouble, but Reva put him in his place. I hope we don't have to see him again, but he looks like the type to fish around for trouble."

"Yikes, I'm sorry to hear about that. Was he the one with the leather jacket?"

"Precisely."

"Yeah, I saw him bossing everyone around out there. He told the officers to collect samples and evidence, all of that police mumbo-jumbo."

"My friend, I don't know what you mean by that word."

"Oh! Sorry, my man." Rory chuckled, slapping Cyrus on the arm. "Sometimes I forget that you died in the 19th century. That feels like prehistoric times to me."

"I do read to catch up with the times. Some words slip past me, I'm afraid," he replied. Glancing at Reva, Cyrus noticed that she hadn't said a word. "Are you feeling alright?"

She looked up from the crack in the counter that she stared at. Realizing that he was talking to her, Reva managed a quick smile and firm nod.

"Of course. I just…" Her limbs still felt weak, thinking about the investigation. "I need to go talk with my aunt. I feel like checking up on her."

"Good on you for sticking by your family!" Rory commended. "It's nice to have someone look after you from time to time, you know?"

"Before you go." Cyrus reached out and gently grabbed her arm, staring up at the second floor. "Rory and I were just discussing a strange smell that we sensed in one of the hallways upstairs. I wanted to let you know about it."

"It was pretty gnarly, Reva."

"Gnarly?" Cyrus repeated. "I don't think I've heard of that one, either."

"Man, you need to start watching some reality TV or something."

"A smell?" Reva wrinkled up her nose. "I-I'll handle it later, but thank you for telling me. It's probably one of the ventilation shafts that isn't circulating air properly."

"I assumed the same," Cyrus replied, placing his hands behind his back. "I try to make sure the hotel is spotless nine times out of ten, you know that."

"Did anyone tell you that your outfit looks especially clean today?" Rory commented, staring at Cyrus' attire that was straight out of Victorian-era England. "I'm jealous."

"Clean? I always make sure my clothes are washed."

"I didn't mean *that* sort of clean, but it's okay."

"We have to continue our conversation over some tea, my friend. You need to teach me more about this modern way of speaking. I've turned a blind eye to it for too long."

"Sure thing!"

Leaving the ghosts to their own devices, Reva hurried out of *The Dimidio Inn* and towards her old Jeep Wrangler that she inherited from her father. One step out the door and she nearly tripped over Pistol, who scurried across her path.

"Hey!" Reva exclaimed. "What's up with you?"

"Wherever you're going, can I come with you?" Pistol pleaded. "I'm tired of these cops disturbing my sleep and ruining my fur! *Two* of them tried to pet me and I sent both of them back where they came from. They know better than to mess with me."

28

Reva rolled her eyes, scooping up her kitten with a hand.

"Sure you did, bud. But I'm sure they were just cowering with fear at the sight of you."

Chapter 5

"Everything looks normal," Reva said.

She strode briskly through the woods with Pistol trotting at her heels. Her Auntie Alva lived in a wilder part of town where there were more trees than houses. Reva had always loved visiting the cozy home that Alva's family had owned since before she was born. It was the site of many fond memories from Reva's childhood and she wanted to make many more.

Hopefully this wouldn't turn out to be an unpleasant memory.

As she hurried up the path, she tried to take note of anything amiss. The hearty vegetable patch looked healthy with no signs of distress. There were no footprints or signs of extra tire tracks on the drive.

"Looks like we beat Matt Carver," Reva said to Pistol.

"Only one way to find out," Pistol said.

Without bothering to knock, Reva threw open the door.

"Auntie Alva? Auntie Alva, where are you?"

"What are you yelling about?"

Reva tumbled into the living room and gasped with relief to see the familiar form of her aunt. Alva sat propped up her rocking chair in front of the fireplace, a bundle of knitting in her lap. It looked like there was a new sweater on her needles. There was still a small fire going even though it was seasonably warm outside.

Reva felt another surge of determination to protect her family.

"What happened?" Reva demanded.

"Hello Reva," Auntie Alva said calmly. "Why don't you take your shoes off and sit down? Hello, Pistol."

While Reva toed her shoes off, Pistol scampered across the room and leapt into Auntie Alva's lap.

"You can't help with my knitting," Auntie Alva told him.

"I don't know why you won't let me," Pistol said. "I have many more needles."

"Needle-sharp claws, you mean," Auntie Alva chuckled.

"Same diff."

"Pistol, this is serious," Reva snapped. "Auntie Alva, what were you thinking leaving those signs at the cemetery about Burton Crabb?"

Auntie Alva frowned, puzzled.

"How did you know it was me?"

Reva rolled her eyes.

"I would recognize that handwriting anywhere," she said. "Luckily I don't think anyone else has figured it out yet."

"What do you mean?" Auntie Alva paused her knitting to pay more attention to Reva. "Why should I care if anyone knows that I wrote those signs? I had a perfectly good reason."

At those words, Reva felt the tension in her stomach ease a little.

"I knew there had to be," she said. "Why'd you put up the signs?"

"Because he has to be stopped," she said simply. "He's a nuisance, I didn't want him in the cemetery with his silly tours anymore."

"They were pretty silly," Pistol said dryly.

"Who cares," Reva said. "Don't you think a sign like that was a little extreme?"

"Burton Crabb was spreading lies about the deceased," Auntie Alva said grimly. "His so-called 'true' tours were packed with sensationalized embellishments. It was an embarrassment. And on top of that." She gestured with a knitting needle.

"He let his tour groups trash the place. The other day, I had to pick up a whole bag of takeout containers and a newspaper. It was too much."

Reva had to admit that her auntie had a point.

"What would you have done in my place?" Auntie Alva asked.

"I don't know, maybe talk to him?"

"Ha!" Auntie Alva laughed. "And have him deny everything and then make false promises to change? I'll spare myself."

"I can confirm, he was just that slimy," Pistol said.

"Fine," Reva said. "Just promise me you had nothing to do with his murder."

Auntie Alva's jaw went slack. Her face went pale and her knitting drooped limply in her lap.

"He's dead?" she asked, her voice hoarse with shock.

"Shot with an arrow," Reva whispered.

"Oh my, how horrible." Auntie Alva's ball of yarn dropped to the floor and rolled away. When she didn't acknowledge it, Pistol leapt after it.

Reva felt confident that she knew her aunt better than anyone in the world. It seemed clear that Alva was genuinely stunned to learn about Crabb's death. Either that or she was hiding something for her niece for the first time in her life.

Reva didn't even want to consider that, but the idea refused to leave her head: her Auntie Alva, the only family she had left, involved in something so terrible.

The image of Crabb's body wrapped in a sheet in the cemetery filled her mind. It was easy to imagine the arrow thudding into his chest, the blood staining his clothes, and her aunt holding the bow.

Just the idea of it made her sick to her stomach.

She closed her eyes and tried to force down the nausea. Sweat broke out on her upper lip and she shuddered. Just then, a tiny, sharp pain on her ankle made her jump in surprise.

Pistol crouched by her feet, about to sink his claws into her flesh for the second time.

"Pull yourself together," he hissed. "This isn't helping anyone."

Reva nodded rapidly. Auntie Alva couldn't possibly be involved in a murder, even someone as unsavory as Burton Crabb. She couldn't shoot a bow for one thing. And she just couldn't kill anyone.

"Sorry," she said, but Auntie Alva still seemed in shock at the news. Even though she hated to see her aunt in pain, Alva's reaction did cement Reva's belief in her innocence.

"Auntie Alva?" she asked hesitantly.

"I'm sorry," Auntie Alva said. "Just taking it in."

"Well, now we've got a criminal on the loose."

"Do they think it's me? Because of the signs?"

"No," Reva said at once, trying to sound convincing. "But the real killer is still out there. You knew Burton better than I did. Did he have any enemies? Someone who might have wanted him dead."

Pistol trotted across the carpet with Auntie Alva's ball of yarn tucked carefully in his mouth. He offered it to her and she took it to resume knitting.

"Let's see," she said over the gentle clacking of her needles. "I only knew him professionally. Only wanted to know him professionally. Really, any amount of time spent with that man was too much, if you ask me."

Reva winced in agreement.

"I know he's dead now and that's probably insensitive of me to say, but it's the truth." Auntie Alva said with a shrug.

"It's okay. Are you sure you can't think of anyone?" Reva asked.

"I didn't say I couldn't think of anyone," Auntie Alva said. "I saw his tours come through our cemetery all the time.

34

Mostly he did them all himself, but he did have some other folks working for him.

"I seem to remember a young woman who ran some of the tours and hated his guts. I think she'd been dating him until he double-crossed her to get ahead."

"What was her name?" Pistol asked.

Auntie Alva tapped her needs together as she thought.

"Brenda something?"

"Brenda Braceling?" Reva had seen her around town.

"That's it," Auntie Alva confirmed. "I'd hate to accuse anyone, but she certainly seemed to have a motive."

"Even if she had nothing to do with it, she still might know something," Reva said eagerly. "We'll go talk to her."

She leapt to her feet, already more optimistic than when she'd arrived. Having a plan of action gave her a sense of purpose and made her feel less helpless.

"Be careful you two," Auntie Alva started to say, but she was interrupted by a sharp knock at her door.

"Are you expecting someone?" Reva asked as Auntie Alva tucked away her needles and went to the door.

When she opened it, Matt Carver was standing on the porch, already holding out his gold badge.

"Good afternoon, ma'am," he said. "I'm Detective Carver."

"What are you doing here?" Reva spat.

Matt looked over Auntie Alva's shoulder and glared at Reva.

"I think I could ask you the same question."

"I'm just paying a friendly visit to my aunt. Is it still legal to visit a family member?"

"Not right now," Matt said. He turned back to Auntie Alva. "I'm sorry, ma'am, I'm afraid I need you to come down to the station."

Reva went rigid. It was like a nightmare come to life.

"We need to ask you some questions about Burton Crabb's murder," Matt went on. "I can give you a ride in my car."

"Am I accused of anything, Detective?" Auntie Alva asked.

"I'm afraid I'm not at liberty to say," Matt said stiffly.

Reva felt her blood boil, there was no way he'd take her aunt away without a fight.

Chapter 6

"Listen," Reva said, stepping between her aunt and the detective. She jabbed her finger into his chest. "I know that you're just trying to do your job, but I would really appreciate it if you didn't do this to my aunt right now. It's not right."

36

"Let the man do his duty, my dear," Aunt Alva interjected, rather exasperated. "The sooner we get this done, the sooner everything will pass over us like a dark cloud. Don't worry your little head about it."

Matt smiled, bowing his head respectfully towards the elderly woman.

"Thank you for your cooperation and wise words, ma'am. It's refreshing to hear."

Reva glared at him for that comment. She softened when she turned towards her aunt again, leaning close and keeping her voice low.

"Aunt Alva, are you sure about this? Do you really think you can trust this man?"

"I don't see a reason why I shouldn't," she replied, cupping Reva's face. "You worry too much about me. If you keep it up, you're going to start growing white hairs like little old me!"

Both Matt and Aunt Alva chuckled at the comment. Reva responded with a bewildered look. Her auntie was taking this *way* too calmly. Meanwhile, Reva worked up a storm at the mere thought of her aunt getting taken in for interrogation.

"Before he takes you," she said, moving herself between the detective and her aunt once more. "I just want to ask the reason for this. I feel like I have the right to know."

Leaning on the doorway, Matt sighs. He fetched his sunglasses from one of his jacket pockets, placing the lenses securely atop his head. Reva fought against the urge to roll her eyes.

"We have eyewitness testimony who says they saw Miss Alva Brennan setting up those signs on the cemetery entrance a few days before the murder occurred. For that reason, I need to speak with your aunt formally and ask her a few questions about what happened."

Reva opened her mouth to interject, but Matt beat her to it.

"She's not being accused of anything, just so you know." Shifting her gaze towards Aunt Alva, he grinned. "Once again, I want to thank you for your cooperation so far. It means a lot."

"Honey, ask all the questions you want. I just want to get back to my knitting."

"Auntie Alva!" Reva exclaimed. "You're really just going to go with him? No questions asked?"

"She knows I mean no harm," he said. "I'm glad to know that there's someone in the Brennan family who does."

"You make jabs like that and then wonder why I want nothing to do with you?" Reva grimaced. "You're worse than I thought."

"Ouch." Matt placed a hand over his heart. "What am I going to do now?"

"Reva!" Aunt Alva grabbed her by the wrist, knitting her brows together. "You don't usually act this way in front of people. What's happening with you?"

"That's news to me," Matt chimed.

"I don't like his type," Reva huffed. "Quite frankly, I don't think he's trustworthy and I worry about letting him take you away to the police station. He has annoyed me enough for one day."

"And to think, I thought I was getting somewhere with you." Matt shrugged, pushing off the doorway. "That's alright. I'm sorry that I've annoyed you so badly, I didn't mean to."

She closed her eyes and shook her head. "Please stop talking."

"Will do. Miss Alva, will you please follow me out to my vehicle? I've parked it over there."

"Reva, don't worry about anything. I'll be fine," Aunt Alva whispered, kissing her niece's temple. "And try to be a little nicer to this gentleman, will you? I think it would serve you well to have him as an ally rather than an enemy."

"I disagree, Auntie," Reva replied softly, watching as Aunt Alva followed Matt out to his large SUV with black-tinted windows.

Pistol nudged his head against her legs. The two of them watched despondently as Matt opened the passenger seat door for Aunt Alva to climb in. Then, he hurried to the other side of the vehicle to hop into the driver's seat. It didn't take long for them to zoom out of the area, leaving behind a cloud of dust in their trail.

"I'm so sick of that guy," Reva said eventually, stalking into the cottage and slamming the door. "I don't know how he does it, but every time I see him, I get a sour feeling in my stomach. It's horrible."

"Sheesh," Pistol responded. "I've never seen someone tick you off this badly. I mean, sure. The guy is annoying, but he's someone you have to brush off like those pesky little flies that get in your ears. You know?"

"I appreciate your pep talk, Pistol, but that's not what I need right now." Reva plopped down upon the couch. Leaning forward, she ran her hand through her hair, clutching at her scalp. "He just took away my aunt."

"Don't you think you're blowing this whole thing out of proportion?" Pistol hopped beside her, nudging at her arm to get her to look at him. "Alva will be back soon. The guy said that she's not being accused of anything, so it's unlikely that they will keep her there longer than necessary."

"He doesn't *like* me," she persisted. "He doesn't trust me, either. I doubt he'll treat my aunt fairly because of that."

40

"Oh, c'mon, Reva." Pistol rubbed at his nose. "He's a detective. I'm sure he's got a moral code."

"I wouldn't be surprised if he were one of those dirty detectives who doesn't mind framing people if it meant getting credit for an investigation," she grumped, staring down at her feet. "I won't let him take out his revenge on my aunt. He can do his best with me, but I refuse to let him mess with her."

Pistol huffed out a breath. Sometimes, he just didn't know what to do with Reva. She could act like a worrywart, especially when it came to issues regarding her aunt. The cat didn't blame her, of course. Aunt Alva was the last family Reva had left since her parents died when she was a teenager. She wanted to protect Alva at all costs, but her emotions clouded her logic.

"If Alva doesn't come back, we can go to the station and ask about her status. For now, all we have to do is sit back and wait. It'll do you no good to worry about things in the meantime."

Biting at her nails, Reva considered the familiar's words carefully. After a few moments, she nodded slightly. Pistol rubbed his furry head against her arm, doing his best to appease her.

"I don't think you should be meddling around in police business, you know," he admitted quietly, glancing up at her with his big gray eyes. "The detective might have you beat on that one."

Reva scoffed.

"I'm not doing anything wrong. I'm just trying to make sure he doesn't bug my aunt unnecessarily. I already failed at that."

"You didn't," Pistol maintained. "He's just asking her some questions. Like a conversation. You can't fault the guy for doing his job."

Reva stared down at the familiar, a gaze laden with curiosity.

"I thought you didn't like him," she said.

"I don't, but he's just trying to figure out who killed that guy. We should just step out of the way and let him do his job. If you don't bug him, he might not bug you." Pistol shrugged. "Or maybe he will. I don't know the guy well enough to make a judgment on his character just yet, and I'll admit he rubbed me the wrong way back at the inn."

"So you're saying we should give him a chance?"

"For now. Until we figure out his true colors." Stretching out his paws, Pistol looked ready for one of his midday naps. "He's a mortal after all, and if he turns out to be a bad apple, well... there's not much he could do to ward off a spell travelling at him at the speed of light."

Laughing, Reva agreed with him on that. She rubbed her eyes, tired from the already-stressful day. She couldn't wait until nightfall, but at the same time, she wondered if she would even get a good night's rest.

"I hope you know that I'm willing to go all-in for my aunt."

"Believe me, I know," Pistol answered. "I'm sure the detective knows that, too."

"And I don't care what that hardhead has to say about it," she said. "Whether he likes it or not, I'm going to figure out the truth on who killed Burton if it's needed to clear my aunt's name. He can cry about that all he wants."

Chapter 7

Just as she anticipated the day prior, Reva didn't get much sleep that night. Her thoughts kept her tossing and turning in bed. Each time she shut her eyes and focused on sleeping, her mind showed it had other plans.

Reva sat up in her bed, glancing at the time. Eight o'clock. Dragging herself out of bed, she decided that she needed to investigate the cause of the maelstrom in her head: Brenda Braceling, the woman Aunt Alva mentioned who had a rocky history with Burton Crabb. An ex-lover who worked for his company. In Reva's eyes, that situation sounded like a simmering volcano on the verge of bursting wide open.

43

Maybe with Burton's sudden death, it had.

She threw on a casual outfit for the day. A plaid shirt over a tank top, followed with some jeans and boots. Grabbing her keys, she made her way out of her bedroom and towards the lobby. There, she spotted Cyrus and Pistol already manning the counter. While the ghost read a short novel, the cat groomed his fur.

"Good morning, you two," she said, less chipper than usual. "I hope you guys had a better night than I did."

"Mine was extravagant, thank you for asking," Pistol replied, lapping at the space between his paws. "You look like a zombie. No offense."

"Thanks so much, Pistol. I love it when you're nice to me."

"Don't mind him," Cyrus said, setting aside his book. "You look stunning, as usual. Did you do something new with your hair? It has a beautiful shine."

"Yeah, probably just hair oil. I haven't washed it in a few days."

Pistol cackled.

"Regardless of that fact, I think you look great."

"Can you cut it out with the flirting, Romeo?" The cat exaggerated a gag. "I already feel a hairball coming up and it's your fault for being so sappy."

"You're as melodramatic as the character you just mentioned." Cyrus looked to Reva. "If you don't mind me asking, where are you going? It's quite early. Have you even had breakfast yet?"

"Nope," she replied, popping the consonant sound. "I don't have much of an appetite right now, but I've been thinking about hash browns for the entire week."

"Would you like me to cook you a batch before you head out?" Cyrus offered, already heading towards the kitchen. "It won't take long I promise."

Pistol stood up on his hind legs, doing his best impression of Cyrus' accent and mannerisms.

"Ah, yes, Reva. Can you come over here and stand oh-so-close to me while I make your food? Would you like some ice cold tea while I'm at it, Your Majesty?" Pistol pranced around on the hotel reception desk for added effect. "When I'm done, can I recite one of my love poems to you while we stargaze beneath the trees?"

Seeing that the kitten was having too much fun with himself, Reva batted him back onto his four legs. Cyrus scoffed, crossing his arms over his chest.

"I don't sound like that."

"The last part appealed to me, so I don't even know why you're trying to make fun of him for that," she said. Cyrus lit up. "Anyways, I'm good with breakfast, Cyrus, but thank you. I need to go talk to some woman that Aunt Alva told me about. Apparently, she used to date Burton and probably had a good reason to see him six feet under."

"Who?" Cyrus frowned. "I hope you're not getting yourself into trouble."

"I doubt it. Her name is Brenda Braceling and she works in *Terror Tales* near the town square. I'm going to drop by and see what information I can pull from her. Hopefully, she'll give me something that leads the investigation away from my aunt and towards literally anyone else."

"What? Are you the lead detective on the case now?" Pistol scoffed. "Did that leather-jacket-sunglasses detective curl up and die already?"

"I'm just trying to speed the process."

"You're sticking your nose in police business when you have other things to worry about," the cat pointed out.

Reva scrunched up her face.

"Like what?"

Just then, one of the upstairs doors slammed shut with a resounding boom, causing the three of them to flinch upright in surprise. Reva groaned, glaring daggers towards that general direction.

"Cyrus, can you tell off whoever slammed that door? That gets annoying quickly."

46

"And that makes two of 'em," Pistol remarked, nodding towards the entrance.

Turning her head, Reva's face soured when she saw the individual standing in her doorway. In a long faux suede jacket, Donna Corona sauntered in, her clacking heels announcing her uninvited presence. Taking off her leopard sunglasses, she studied the lobby with her chin tilted a little higher than usual. She cleared her throat, sending Reva a tight smile.

If there was anyone who rivaled Matt Carver in arrogance in Reva's eyes, it had to be Donna. She was an ambitious banking heiress who never had to work for a penny in her life. Seeing Shadow Woods as an opportunity to make money, Donna wanted to raze the town down to its foundations and build tourist attractions in its stead. Amusement parks, high-scale restaurants, and spa hotels. Things that the locals did *not* need.

Reva could see through the woman like a piece of glass. She wanted *The Dimidio Inn*, but she was going to make sure that Donna didn't get it. Even if she managed to die the next day somehow, Donna would be unable to pry the hotel from her cold, dead hands.

"It's so nice to see you, Reva," Donna said. "I hope you're having a great day so far."

Leaning on the counter, Reva crossed her legs at the ankles. Then, she nodded her head towards Donna.

"Who do you think you're fooling?"

Donna's eyes widened. "I beg your pardon?"

"You're coming into my establishment with a fake smile and obnoxious tone, thinking that I'm going to sell you my family's business for a cheap buck?" Reva shook her head. "You must have lost your mind."

"Now, you're just getting ahead of yourself–"

"I've heard enough from you already," she said, waving her off. "I have errands to run and I don't have the time to deal with your kind."

"People warned me about your character. I didn't expect you to be this bullish, but it seems like the rumors were true." Donna said.

"And that affects me how?"

Hiding her smile, she watched as Cyrus made her way over and blew a quick stream of air into the woman's left air. Donna whipped around in all directions, cupping her ear. "What was that?"

"What was what?" Reva asked. "Now you're just making a fool of yourself."

Donna gritted her teeth. "I just want a simple business negotiation with you! You're only prolonging the inevitable by avoiding this conversation."

"I'm not prolonging anything. You're not going to get my hotel and that's that."

Seeing that the woman was distracted, Pistol hustled over and squatted over her boots. When Donna noticed, she shouted out in fury and disgust. "Your stupid animal just peed on me!"

"I should have done more than that," Pistol shot back, but the woman only heard it as meows. "Last night's dinner was ready to come out, too."

Reva grabbed Donna by the wrist, dragging her out of the lobby despite the woman's snorts and empty threats of a lawsuit. Once they were outside, Donna snatched her arm away, smoothing out the jacket's fabric.

"You shouldn't pick fights that you have no chance of winning," Reva said.

Laughing dryly, Donna's expression soon morphed into a scowl. "I've won challenges before. You're nothing new to me."

"You're wrong, but I'll let you think that."

"That's what they all say in the beginning," she jeered. "They never last. The world revolves on money, after all."

Turning away, Donna walked towards her convertible. Unable to stop herself, Reva mumbled a spell that caused a sudden force to hit Donna in the back of her knees.

She stumbled over, yelling out as she crashed into the ground. The collision caused her sunglasses to fly from her grasp, shattering against the gravel below.

Reva hissed in a breath. "You should be careful next time," she called out to the woman. "That was a nasty fall."

"Be quiet!" Donna snapped, glaring at her. The woman's blonde curls were disheveled and her green eyes burned with fury. "Did you push me?!"

"Don't be silly. I didn't move from this spot."

With that, Reva hid a smile and returned to the inn.

Chapter 8

Humming a radio tune as she parked her car, Reva spotted the *Terror Tales* building on the other side of the street. It was a modest, one-story brick structure with the company's name in bold letters across a white background. It didn't command too much attention when compared to the other businesses on the same block, but it had its charm. Her old car rumbled as she turned the key, shutting off the ignition.

She hurried toward the front entrance and peered through the glass doors. At first glance, she didn't see anyone inside. It was strangely quiet. She took some time to observe the lobby, a white-tiled floor accompanied by beige walls, and an empty front desk with a multitude of documents scattered across the surface. Beyond the desk, she spotted a row of offices. Seeing that there was no one there to receive her or ask her business, Reva invited herself in.

After observing the numerous name plaques attached to the office doors, she finally found the one which interested her the most. *Brenda Braceling*. With the office door slightly ajar, Reva could hear fragments of the conversation being had inside. She leaned on the wall, tuning in.

"...So what do you think? Do you think this is a possibility for you and your company?"

"Why, uh, yes. I believe so, ma'am. Now that we're going to be transferring under new leadership due to the... untimely departure of my boss, we can consider your demands." A chair scooted forward. "Just so you know, I've been trying to promote the truth on these tours for a while now. I never had the chance until now."

"That's refreshing to hear. What happened?"

"The old boss liked to embellish stories in order to capture the public's attention and try to rake in more reservations. In doing so, he often made up lies about the deceased–"

"Hmm. That's what he did to my great-grandmother."

"Indeed. I'm sorry about that."

"You're going to fix things, right?" Someone's foot tapped against the floor. "All the lies he used to say about my

great-grandmother… Will your company stop doing that?
Please?"

"I assure you, Ms. Owens, that from now on, our
company will do nothing but promote the truth during our
ghost tours. Out of respect for the deceased and their loved
ones, I'll handle that."

"Good." Ms. Owens sighed. "That's great to hear.
What your boss used to do… To put it simply, it created a lot
of stress for myself and my family. I mean, making up the lie
that she was an insane person who poisoned her husband's
mistresses? Really?"

"My apologies, Ms. Owens, our company really
intended no harm–"

"You caused a lot of it!" the woman snapped.

An uncomfortable silence followed, which made
Reva recoil slightly at the sudden change in her tone.
However, the woman soon calmed down.

"I-I'm sorry about that, I didn't mean to shout at
you…"

"It's alright, Ms. Owens. I understand how you're
feeling. Rest assured, things will change around here moving
forward."

"Thank you." Sniffling followed. "You have no idea
how much this means to me and my family. We greatly
appreciate your efforts."

"No worries, ma'am. I'm just trying to do the right thing. Tissue?"

"Ah, thank you." Then, she blew her nose. "Sorry to take up so much of your time. I didn't expect to be here for so long."

"I'm happy that we managed to come to a satisfying resolution, Ms. Owens. Thank you for stopping by and I hope you advertise *Terror Tales* to your friends and loved ones in the future."

"Mm. I think the wound is still too fresh to do that just yet, but I'll think about it. Thank you!" The chair scooted backwards. "Oh! Before I forget. Would you like one of these? I coach the high school softball team and we made these bracelets for a recent fundraiser."

"I'd love one, thank you." Reva heard scuffling sounds as the women exchanged money.

Suddenly, the door opened. The person exiting the office wore a white sweatshirt and khaki shorts, along with sneakers and socks that rode up to her calves. *Shadow Woods High* was printed across the front. Nearly bumping into Reva, the woman gasped.

"Oh, I'm so sorry! Were you waiting for Brenda?"

"Yes, actually, but no worries. I didn't wait too long."

"I believe I've seen you around town before. I love your hair! Is that your natural color?"

Reva nodded.

"It's absolutely beautiful. Take care now!"

Smiling, Reva watched as the woman took off. She reminded Reva of those soccer moms with the big minivans that drove the neighborhood kids around to their afternoon games.

Heading inside the office, she caught Brenda organizing the papers on her desk. The woman sent her a tired grin.

"Hello there. Can I help you?"

"I actually wanted to speak to you. I'm sorry if I had to make an appointment in advance for that sort of thing."

"No, not at all!" Brenda gestured towards the seat in front of her desk. "Please, sit. What's your name?"

"Reva Brennan. I own *The Dimidio Inn* on the other side of town."

"Oh! I've heard about that inn! It's right next to *The Yews* which is a popular spot for most of our tours."

"I know," she replied. "I think I've seen you guys pass through the cemetery once or twice before. My aunt and I would appreciate it if you could police your tour groups a little more."

Brenda frowned.

"In what way?"

"Sometimes, the tourists leave litter on the ground. We try to keep the cemetery tidy because it's supposed to be a place to pay your respects, you know? Seeing a bunch of trash on the ground, near the gravesites, is off-putting and borderline disrespectful."

"I understand, Ms. Brennan. Thank you for bringing this to my attention." Brenda worked quickly, typing these notes down on her computer. "I assure you that our tour guides will be mindful of this in the future."

Gazing at the bracelet hanging around one of her pens, Reva felt intrigued by the creative design. By the looks of it, the departed woman made the bracelets out of phone wires, intertwined with one another tightly to make a vibrant and original decoration. Brenda's had a nice pink and black color combination.

"Was that all you wanted to speak about, Ms. Brennan?"

Looking up, Reva realized that she'd nearly dozed off for a second. Lack of sleep would do that to anyone, she figured.

"Actually, that's not the reason why I came here."

Brenda raised a brow, leaning forward in her seat.

"Well, I'm all ears for whatever you have to say. Does it relate to the quality of our tours in any way?"

"It involves your old boss, actually. Burton Crabb."
Reva cleared her throat, leaning on the armrest of the seat.
"You see, I'm in a tough situation right now. I'm sure you've
heard that he's been murdered and his body was found in *The
Yews*."

Brenda froze up, mouth falling open, and eyes
widening significantly. She eventually responded to Reva's
words with a small nod. She'd heard, apparently, but still
looked shocked and horrified.

"Unfortunately, my aunt got caught up in that mess
unnecessarily based on a misunderstanding, but she mentioned
that you might have some important knowledge about the
whole situation. Considering that you and Burton had a
romantic relationship at one point or another, you're in the
best position to know about the people who might have a
vendetta against him."

"I... I mean..." Brenda stammered.

"I just wanted to ask if you knew anything that could
help clear my aunt's name. There's no pressure, of course, but
anything would help. I'm working with limited time, so I kind
of need this information urgently."

"Ma'am, I-I don't think this is the most appropriate
time or place for such matters..."

"Why not?" Reva pressed. "It's a simple question,
really. You just need to tell me about the people who would

have benefited from seeing Burton Crabb shot with an arrow through the chest."

Brenda swallowed thickly. Reva continued.

"Maybe a business rival that wanted to surpass *Terror Tales*? A vindictive family member who wanted to see him fail?" Reva loosened up, staring at the trembling woman before her. "Or maybe even an ex-lover whose relationship failed due to unknown reasons?"

Brenda's hand clenched around her armrest. Small veins popped out along her knuckles.

"So?" Reva gestured towards her. "Do you know anything about that?"

"I don't know," Brenda started, wetting her chapped lips. "I don't think I know anything that would be useful to you–"

"I'm sure you do, Brenda," she interjected, causing the woman to flinch. "Please. Tell me everything you know about the situation and I *might* overlook the fact that your business has been perpetuating lies about our community for years now."

Chapter 9

"Ms. Brennan–"

"Call me Reva. That title makes me feel much older than I already am."

57

"O...kay. Reva. I'm not sure I'm the one who can help you."

"Of course you are," she said. "All I'm trying to do is clear my aunt's name and get her out of this horrible situation. *You* can provide me with the information I need to do so. Am I right or am I right?"

"No." Brenda shook her head. "I-I truly don't know anything."

"Nothing?" Reva didn't sound too convinced. "No enemies that placed a target on Burton's back? He didn't owe debts to anyone?"

"Not that I know of, no."

"Then let's talk about the relationship you had with him." Reva rested her chin upon her closed fist. "Go on. Tell me why you broke up."

"Ms. Brennan, this is very inappropriate."

"Brenda, I really need you to cooperate because I didn't have the best morning and I don't have the patience to have you dodge my questions. Did things end amicably between the two of you?"

Leaning back in her chair, Brenda sighed as she gazed upon the framed paintings on her wall. She tapped her manicured fingernail upon her desk.

"Not really."

"What happened? I'm not saying you did anything." Reva raised her hands up. "I'm just interested in knowing the nature of your relationship with him. That's all."

"Will this *help* you and your aunt in any way?" Brenda asked, glaring at Reva. "It doesn't seem like it."

"Maybe it will," she replied. "Maybe, whatever you tell me can help bring me in the right direction. Don't you want to find the person who killed your ex?"

"No." Brenda toyed with the pen on her desk. "In all honesty, I think they just did the town a huge favor. You said it yourself. *Terror Tales* doesn't have too good of a reputation in Shadow Woods anymore. Burton made sure of that."

"Was he the one spreading lies about all the deceased people?" Reva narrowed her eyes. The thought of someone disrespecting the dead sent shivers down her spine. After all, they had multiple ways to come back and set things straight.

"Yes, he did. I tried to talk to him about it. We had received complaints before, since people were horrified that he was saying ridiculous things about their family members, their ancestors…" Brenda raised her hand, gesturing towards the open door. "I mean, just right now, Natalie Owens came to me to complain about that. She said that Burton described her great-grandmother as a lovesick, infatuated wife who killed her husband's mistresses as a way to get him to stay with her. Who does that?"

59

"I overheard that," Reva admitted, fiddling with her thumbs. "You're going to right his wrongs, at least. That's admirable."

"Yeah. I guess so." Brenda mindlessly clicked her nails on her desktop, mainly as a way to keep her idle hands busy. "When I dated him, I... I *tried* to get him to listen. The idiot never would. He always belittled me for wanting to tell the truth. I couldn't stand it."

In recollecting her memories, Brenda accidentally knocked over her coffee mug, spilling its contents all over the floor. As she leaned over to handle the mess, she caused the neatly stacked pile of documents to scatter. Her cheeks reddened, realizing the disaster she made.

Reva stood from her seat, helping her collect the papers. Brenda mumbled a quick thank you as she dumped a pile of paper napkins onto the floor, spreading them out unevenly to soak up the brown liquid staining the white floors. The scent of coffee wafted through her office, the only bright side of the situation.

"You're nervous," Reva commented, once she returned to her seat. "I'm sorry if talking about him makes you feel this way."

Sighing, Brenda cleaned her sticky hands with the last napkin that remained.

"It's fine. The past is past, right?" She managed a weak grin. It didn't last very long. "I don't like talking about him. In hindsight, it's so strange to me why I was interested in him in the first place."

Reva laughed.

"That's how it works once you've broken up with someone. The rose-colored glasses come off."

"Exactly. He had some shady business practices that *horrify* me now that I think about it with a clear mind, but I was willing to look past that for the sake of our relationship. If I could smack the me from five months ago, I would."

"You're not alone." Reva folded her hands over her lap. "I've had a few people who've made me feel the same way. It's eye-opening, in a way."

"Anyways." Brenda tossed the napkin she used into the trash beside her desk. "We broke up and that was that. He still kept me around, surprisingly."

"I can tell why. It looks like you're the one handling all the problems around here."

"Sure. He was too much of a coward to face an angry customer so he used me as his shield." Brenda rolled her eyes at the memory. "He didn't mind yelling in my face, though. What a bum. He moved on quickly after me. Last I heard, he was trying to date some girl who was into archery. I can't remember her name."

Reva sat on the edge of her seat with this new information.

"Do you know where she works?"

"No, I'm sorry. I'd tell you if I did. I don't know if she and Burton ever had something serious, but he mentioned her in passing once. Maybe as a way to get a rise out of me, I don't know. He was silly like that."

"Silly." Reva repeated. "I had other descriptors in my mind, but sure."

A knock came on the open door. Underneath the doorway, a woman with a blonde bob stood with a white collared shirt and a black pencil skirt. She chewed loudly on some bubblegum, popping bubbles occasionally. The name tag on her shirt read *Lola Gooden*.

"Sorry to interrupt your chat, Brenda, but we've got an important visitor out front. He's asking for some information about our old boss. I tried looking, but I don't know where to find where he kept those things."

Reva caught the subtle Boston accent on Lola's words.

"Was he asking for records of some kind?" Brenda asked.

"Yeah! Records of all of Burton's recent tours and all the people who went with him. Plus their contact information." Lola popped a quick bubble. "It's a lot to ask for, I know."

"Don't worry about it." Scooting back in her chair, Brenda started looking through her cabinet files. She was careful not to roll her chair into the coffee-stained mess she created moments prior. "And did he say why he wanted these records? Who's the person asking for all this, anyway?"

"Beats me. He looks intimidating, though. He's got some of those aviator shades. My pa used to wear 'em when he worked as a co-pilot."

"A detective?" Reva asked, turning around in her seat.

"Yeah, I think so! He flashed some bright yellow badge before asking me all these things."

Oh no, she thought, tensing up in her seat. *Why did he have to come here?*

"He's probably here to investigate Burton's murder case," Brenda reasoned, taking out multiple manila folders from her four drawer cabinet file. "Kind of like you, Reva. Only more official."

"Really?" Lola chewed loudly on her gum. "You're an investigator, too?"

"No, not at all. I just want to clear my auntie's name. Thanks to Brenda, I think I have the information to start doing that."

"Aw, Brenda, look at you! You're a good Samaritan." Lola rested her hand over Brenda's once she reached over to retrieve the files, squeezing gently. "Things will start changing around here now that you're taking charge."

Reva's eyes widened, staring up at Brenda. With Burton's death, she suddenly assumed a more important role in the company. Did that mean…?

"Excuse me, ma'am." A man's voice called out from the front of the building. "Do you have the files I'm asking for? If not, that's alright."

"No, no, sir! I've got 'em right here, don't you worry!" Lola hurried over back to the front desk.

Rising from her seat, Reva peeked her head out of the office to see if what she was thinking was true. Sure enough, standing in front of Lola, Detective Matt Carver stood waiting for the records on Burton's ghost tours. He smiled, accepting the folders from Lola before skimming through them.

While doing so, he briefly glanced up from his reading and caught a sight of Reva staring right at him. He returned the gaze, his shades slipping further down his nose.

Chapter 10

At this rate, Reva didn't know if she would ever catch a break. It wasn't even noon yet, and she'd had to deal with Donna Corona and Matt Carver within hours of each other. Her stomach twisted up in disgust as she watched the detective shove the folders underneath his arm and approach her. He took off his sunglasses.

"Why are you here?"

Reva shrugged, still trying to come up with a reasonable response.

"I just wanted to stop by."

"That's awfully suspicious. What business do you have with this company? Are you trying to meddle in police affairs again?"

"Huh?" Reva scrunched up her face in confusion. "I haven't meddled in anything. Besides, I don't have to explain anything to you. What I do isn't your business."

"Not when you're sticking your nose in my investigation."

Brenda and Lola stood to the side, eyes flickering between the two as they argued outside of the offices. Leaning over, Brenda whispered to Lola to keep searching in her office for more of Burton's records. She nodded, hurrying in.

"What happened with my aunt's interrogation yesterday? You let her go, right? Dropped her off safely back at her cottage?"

"You can ask her yourself. What your aunt did after the interrogation is not my concern."

"So you'll stop bothering her, right? Now that you've asked your pointless questions? She wasn't the one who killed Burton. You and I both know that."

"That's something I have yet to make a final conclusion on," Matt replied, readjusting his grip on the files. "If I need any more clarification from her, I'll make sure to get it."

"No." Reva shook her head. "You need to leave her alone. I don't want you bothering her anymore."

"You know, I'm starting to get the strange feeling that you're *impeding* my ability to conduct a fair investigation. What's that about? Now I can't interrogate one of the suspects because it hurts your feelings? I'm not going to cave in just because you're kicking and screaming about it."

Narrowing her eyes, she felt the apples of her cheeks start to burn red. The tips of her ears soon followed as her breathing turned quick and shallow.

"Uh, I'm sorry to interrupt." Brenda said, lifting up a finger and stepping between the two. "We're not the only ones in the building, you see. Other people are working and we should really keep our voices down."

"My apologies, ma'am," Matt replied. "I never meant for such a disturbance. Then again, I didn't expect to bump into a massive inconvenience here."

66

Reva laughed dryly, hoping that she could blink away the angry tears that started to muddle her vision. That was the last thing she wanted to do in front of the detective. He would never let her live it down, she knew it.

"You never answered my question, by the way." Matt stared at her, studying each feature of her face. His intense glare made her fidget. "What are you doing here?"

"I spoke to Brenda about the state of *The Yews* and what's going to happen with the tours moving forward. I complained about past tourists leaving behind litter and dirtying the cemetery, but she reassured me that things would change from now on."

Nodding to affirm, Brenda smiled awkwardly beside Reva. She wrung her hands together, peeking into her office to see Lola still shuffling through mountains of documents and files.

"Anything else you spoke to her about?"

Brenda glanced at Reva, gnawing on her bottom lip.

"Personal things, but not much else," Reva replied indifferently. "Are you going to stop accusing me of interrupting your investigation now? I just came here to run an errand after all."

"Uh huh."

"Are you looking for potential suspects by looking through Burton's past tourist registration lists? If you are, I suggest finding someone who's able to manipulate a bow and arrow."

Matt sniffed loudly, averting his gaze.

"That information is classified and I can't discuss it openly with civilians."

"I'm just offering you a suggestion."

"I don't need it," he spoke brusquely, which made Brenda take a few steps back. At that point, Reva realized she'd grown used to his strong tone and curt demeanor. "You should stop doing this if you know what's good for you. That's my suggestion to you."

Reva scoffed, resting her hands on her hips. "That's the lousiest suggestion you could have given me."

"Talking to you is like talking to a brick wall."

"I'm not going to step aside and bow down to you just because you're a new detective with a shiny badge that you flash around to get what you want. You're going after my aunt and think I'm just going to let it happen? You must have lost it."

"How annoying can you be?" he mumbled. "You're not going to let me do my job in peace, are you?"

"So as long as you leave my aunt out of this, we're not going to have any issues." Reva tapped against her temple multiple times. "What's not clicking?"

"She is a *suspect*."

"For no good reason," Reva retorted. "She left some signs for Burton telling him to stay out of the cemetery. That constitutes murder, in your eyes?" She gestured towards Brenda. "I just spoke with this woman about the issues his tours caused in the cemetery! That's what my aunt was worried about!"

"If that was the case, then I'm sure I'll reach that conclusion once the investigation comes to an end. For now, I have to keep looking at all the available evidence."

"Who else is a suspect?" Reva asked. She raised a brow when Matt didn't give her an immediate answer. "You don't have anyone else, huh? That's why you're chasing around my aunt like a fly?"

"I don't have time for this." Matt pushed his way past the two women, sticking his head into Brenda's office. "Do you have those last documents or not? I can't stand around here and wait all day."

"No worries, sir, I think I've found what you need," Lola called out from her knees, scooping up the papers clumsily. Pushing herself to stand, she made her way over with the documents. "Some coffee got on them. Brenda, what happened by your desk? Why are my hands so sticky?"

"I spilled some coffee on accident," she replied. "It's not a huge deal, but you stained all those papers, I'm afraid."

"Oops." Lola chewed on her gum, clasping her hands together as the detective grimaced at the documents. "Sorry about that, Detective. The text is still readable, though, so you shouldn't have an issue."

"Yeah. Thanks." Matt shoved them into a folder. "I may have to come back for more information in the future, just so you ladies know."

"I hope those papers can lead you towards the actual killer," Reva chimed in, earning yet another sour glare. "You're stopped at a dead-end if you continue thinking that my aunt had anything to do with it."

"I'll probably consider her the prime suspect at this point."

"What?!" Reva exclaimed. "Why would you do that?"

"You're obstructing the investigation to a point where I'm starting to feel suspicious. For all I know, you could be covering up for your aunt. After speaking to her, I'd like to believe this isn't true, but anything's possible."

"I always knew you were corrupt," she spat. "You're accusing an innocent woman of murder. I hope you consider what you're doing very carefully."

"Don't tell me what to do," Matt said. "It's not going to change my mind each time you yap about it."

Gritting her teeth and feeling the tears start to form, Reva pushed her way out of the building and out towards the street. She hurried towards her car, furiously wiping away at her eyes. She jabbed her keys in the ignition, not even giving her vehicle a few seconds to warm up before zooming off. Acknowledging that she wasn't in the right state of mind, Reva decided to head towards the one place where she could reflect on her situation without disturbances.

Shadow Woods forest bordered the town on the western edge, the origin behind the town's name. Some parts were used for hiking trails and camping while other, more secluded regions, were often dedicated to hunting. Reva focused on the latter, hoping to take her frustrations out in the empty forest without a soul to hear her.

The scream she wanted to expel from her lungs would have probably reached *The Yews*, anyway.

Chapter 11

Large blue orbs expanded out of her palms. Making slashing motions with her arms, Reva shot them against the trunk of an old oak tree, shaking the wooden structure down to its very roots. Groaning loudly, she continued to do so until visible marks started scoring the sides of the oak.

Reva gasped for breath as she leaned on an adjacent tree, observing her aggressive handiwork. Feeling the need to lash out at *something*, she decided that a tree was the best choice. After all, she couldn't just shoot magical projectiles at the mortal detective, no matter how annoying he acted. Neither could she do the same with Donna, who had enough money to bury her in a lawsuit against her if she tried it.

Besides, the town of Shadow Woods didn't know it held witches, or ghosts, or talking cat familiars.

So, she resorted to using her imagination as she struck the tree an untold number of times. Reva thought she was alone in Shadow Woods, but somewhere to her left, high above in the branches, she heard a voice calling out her name.

Looking over, she noticed Cyrus with a book in his hands, seated on a tree branch with one leg dangling freely. He placed a finger between his pages, staring down at her with a grin.

"I implore you not to knock over another tree," he said. "We've already dealt with that ordeal and I don't think you want another mess any time soon."

"Thanks for the advice," she replied, gesturing towards him with a nod. "When did you get here?"

"About an hour ago or so. I noticed that you came and started battling the poor tree over there. I didn't feel like interceding on its behalf."

"It's a good thing you didn't." Reva flexed her fingers. "I needed that."

"Rough day?"

"Where do I ever begin? I wake up after getting little to no sleep to deal with a spoiled banking heiress trying to buy my hotel. Then, I head off to talk to Burton Crabb's ex-girlfriend and Detective Hardhead shows up."

Cyrus frowned, setting down his book once more.

"He keeps telling me to stay out of the investigation, but I just *can't*. Not when my aunt is being wronged by the justice system. I don't want to leave her alone through this process." Reva ran a frustrated hand through her hair, gripping her strands. "I mean, on one hand, I get it. He's doing his job. I think I've acted a bit too childish with him about this situation."

"I believe you've just defended yourself, my beloved." Cyrus readjusted his position on the branch, turning his body to face her directly. "He's conceited and ill-mannered. Your temperament doesn't work well with someone like that."

"Clearly," she whispered. "I just want this investigation to end, but so far, the detective is considering Alva as his main suspect. I doubt he has anyone else in his sights yet."

"Do you?" Cyrus tilted his head. "Has your detective work been more astute than his?"

73

Scratching her head, Reva offered a shy shrug. She couldn't say *that*. After all, the guy had to be good. He was the lead detective in the Shadow Woods Police Department, probably with a few accolades to his name.

However, she couldn't help but wonder if her best friend was onto something.

"Well, I talked to Brenda Braceling. She didn't have the best relationship with Burton. He was her boss and her boyfriend for some time, which made for a really volatile mix."

"Oh, I can only imagine," Cyrus replied, brushing his mustache with his fingers. "You can't get a break from your partner in those situations."

"He wasn't very nice to her. He would spread lies about the dead with his ghost tours and whenever she tried to bring that to his attention, he brushed her off and mistreated her. I don't know how she put up with that for so long. I would have sent a fireball into his nose the first time around."

"Charming response," he said, grinning. "I don't blame you. Do you believe that Brenda had something to do with his death?"

"She might. She also mentioned that Burton had another potential love partner in the mix who was into archery."

"Archery?" Cyrus' eyebrows shot upward. "She sounds like a person more than capable of shooting an arrow through his heart, literally and figuratively. You need to find this woman."

"I agree! The only problem is that I don't know her name, where she works, or what she looks like." Reva sighed. "I just know she exists, which is great and all, but I need to talk to her. My aunt's reputation depends on it."

"Why do you think she killed him?"

"...A crime of passion, maybe? I don't know. Based on what I've heard about him, I don't know *why* these ladies were interested in this man in the first place. He sounds like a piece of work."

"That reminds me of another gentleman we know of."

Cyrus maneuvered himself nimbly to scale down the tree trunk. Reva watched him with crossed arms, impressed by the act. She didn't know how to move as quickly as he did when climbing up and down trees. He looked akin to a lizard.

When his feet landed upon the ground again, Reva smiled. That brought up a thought in her mind.

"Couldn't you just..." Reva pointed from the tree branch to the leaf-covered ground. "Float down or something?"

"Not really, darling. Us spirits still need to adhere to some pesky rules of physics. Though, I admit I'd love to just fly down from the highest tree with ease."

"But you can float upwards, right?"

"To a certain extent, yes. I've tried it before and I reached a height of around eight feet. A force starts pulling me downwards if I try to exceed that threshold."

"Ghosts can walk through objects, too, right?" Reva asked.

"Only objects of a certain width. We'll get lost or disoriented if we try to pass through a giant solid object for too long."

"Feels like only yesterday when I first started learning about this stuff," Reva mused. "It's new to me, but then again, I'm not going to know the precise nature of how it feels to be a ghost until I *become* one. Morbid, but the truth."

"You ask the right questions to propel your learning," Cyrus remarked. "It shows that you have a naturally inquisitive mind."

Cyrus stepped in front of her, taking her by the wrist and twirling her around like a ballroom dancer. Reva nearly toppled over, but enjoyed the small gesture.

"Tell you what. I can see that this issue is going to remain on your mind until you start getting clear answers."

"You know me so well, Cyrus."

76

"We can head to *The Yews* right now and start asking the spirits there for more information. Surely, someone will be able to help us. They chat their heads off all day talking about the news in Shadow Woods."

"Have you been talking with them about the case?"

"Somewhat, but I haven't heard anything that caught my attention. Certain female ghosts keep talking about the detective and how good looking he is." Shuddering, Cyrus didn't try to hide his disgust. "It's such a shame to see them so blinded and lost. I should save them."

"Let them drool over the guy all they want," she replied, waving her hand. "They're dead. What else can they do?"

"I worry about their taste."

"So do I." Reva could admit that Matt was conventionally attractive, but his personality repulsed her. Bright smiles and dazzling eyes could never salvage that. "I hope their gossip leads us somewhere useful."

"It usually does. At the very least, it will bring us on an adventure."

"How is Pistol doing, by the way? He better not be tearing up the place since we're not there."

"Before leaving, I caught him in the forests outside stalking rabbits. He's getting good at that, you know."

Reva and Cyrus entered her car. When she turned on the radio, she watched in amusement as Cyrus listened to the newest pop songs. He could barely understand the vocabulary the singers used, but he liked the rhythm.

"They didn't have this type of music when I was alive. I wish they did! It would have made the parties and balls much more lively."

Reva snorted.

"I can't imagine them playing EDM at a Victorian ball, Cyrus. It probably would have scared the guests."

"It's just something to get used to." Cyrus leaned closer to her, resting his arm on the elbow rest. "On the topic of parties, when will you allow me to take you to one?"

"When this sleepy little town finally decides to have one," she replied, applying some pressure to the gas which caused her car to lurch forward. Cyrus flinched in his seat, which made Reva laugh. "Sorry. It's the music's fault."

Chapter 12

Without the heavy police presence, *The Yews* cemetery finally felt somewhat normal again. The section of the graveyard where they found Burton's corpse was still closed off to the public, but other than that, they could freely pass through the cemetery again.

Dirt paths wound through *The Yews*, guiding individuals towards the gravestones of loved ones to whom they wished to pay respects. Ground lights illuminated these paths when nightfall came. At the center of *The Yews*, a beautiful marble fountain that depicted baby angels spewing water adorned the scene. The donation for the fountain came from one of Reva's ancestors.

Near the back of the cemetery, a large mausoleum stood tall. Inside, the *Spectral Senate* presided. They were a governing body composed of spirits who overlooked mortal and ghost relations. The *Spectral Senate* made sure neither of the two groups overstepped boundaries, for doing so could mean chaos for Shadow Woods.

Reva gazed towards the spot where Burton's body was found. Still closed off to the public. She sighed at the sight. The bright yellow caution tapes were an eyesore.

"I hope they remove those soon," she said to Cyrus, who stood tall at her side. "It probably scares people off once they find out what happened here."

"The police officers gathered their things and left, finally. They were taking up too much space and making it difficult for us to have our normal conversations. Rory told me that the *Spectral Senate* is not at all happy with what happened here."

"That's not surprising. It's pretty easy to make them mad."

"No one is happy, I'm afraid. It feels as if our sanctuary got invaded by unwanted pests. Starting with that detective." Cyrus ran a hand across his clothes, dusting off any lint and smoothing out the wrinkles. "Talking about that man creates an odd sensation in my chest. I can't describe it."

"I already have an idea of what that emotion is."

"Hm?" Cyrus raised his brow. "And what might it be?"

"You should figure that out for yourself," she replied. "It's pretty obvious."

"Not to me!"

Shaking her head, Reva surveyed the graveyard and tried to find someone willing to talk. Other ghosts walked through The *Yews*, chatting idly with one another. Others played games, like flinging balls at each other and catching them. They were careful not to engage in such activities with mortals around, however, just in case one or two could actually see ghosts.

Reva reflected on that. No one, not even the dead, could accurately predict which humans might see ghosts and which might not. The mortal ability to perceive spirits seemed to rely on a mix of genetics, open-mindedness, and sometimes, random talent.

But curiously, most humans could *hear* ghosts. Reva shook her head. So many mysteries existed on both sides of the life-death divide.

Near the fountain, she and Cyrus spotted two twin sister spirits who conversed while dipping their fingers in the water. Polly and Dolly Hannon had been only fifty-six years old when they passed on from their mortal lives due to a tragic car accident. They often wore matching clothes, the only difference being the color. Polly, for instance, sported a pink floral sundress while Dolly wore a light blue one of the same design. They also perched elegant hats upon their blonde heads.

"Come." Reva nudged Cyrus. "We should talk to them."

"Polly and Dolly. Always a delight," Cyrus greeted, widening his arms once he neared. "How have you two wonderful ladies been?"

"Fine," Dolly said.

"We're just discussing some old apple pie recipes we used to make. I'm trying to convince her that we need to make some again! I miss the sweet aroma of my favorite treat."

"It's difficult to find the right ingredients, you know that, Polly." Dolly placed a hand over her sister's knee. "We can always sneak into the nearest grocery store when nightfall comes, but we need to be careful. They have cameras."

"They can't do anything if they see some of their objects floating away," Polly maintained, taking out a small hand fan from her purse. "It's not like they'll croak if they have a few ingredients missing."

"If you'd like, I can stop by the store and fetch you those ingredients," Reva offered with a shrug, smiling at the way the twins lit up at the suggestion. "It wouldn't take much effort on my part."

"Oh, Reva, you're a doll!" Polly exclaimed. "It's a good thing that you've taken good care of *The Dimidio Inn* and *The Yews* ever since your parents died. They used to do the same. Everyone loved them for a reason. We were all heartbroken when they passed."

Dolly nodded. "It was even worse to find out that they died far away from Shadow Woods," she said, frowning. "Their spirits were too distant to come back to *The Yews*. I miss them dearly."

Pressing her lips into a thin line, Reva nodded. Talking about her parents always opened that old wound in her heart that never truly healed. She lost them when she was still only a kid, with no real direction in the world. Thankfully, her Aunt Alva helped her through the darkness and the two of them picked up where her parents left off.

Considering Alva was her mother's older sister, she was particularly devastated to hear about the passing of her younger sibling. Even so, Alva took care of Reva when she could have focused on herself and gave up everything so that Reva could have a better life. Reva knew she wouldn't ever forget that.

"We're sorry to hear about what's happening with Alva," Dolly said, as if she picked up on the energy Reva gave off. "It's a shame that they're accusing her of killing that man. I don't know whose idea it was, but they're obviously mistaken."

"We agree wholeheartedly with that sentiment, Dolly," Cyrus replied, bowing to the seated woman. "The lead detective keeps pestering Reva and Alva about the murder. He doesn't know what he's talking about, I fear."

"Did you know anything about the victim, by the way?" Reva gestured over her shoulder with a thumb. "Burton Crabb? I won't be able to relax until I get my auntie out of this mess. I'm trying to find the killer, for her sake and for the rest of the town."

"What a strong idea," Polly commented, nudging at her sister's side. "There's a murderer on the loose and we don't even know who it is! My, it feels like our town is headed in the wrong direction."

"I hope not," Reva said. "That's why I'm trying to put a stop to things before they spiral out of control. Do you have any information that can help me?"

Dolly leaned over into the fountain, cupping some of the water and watching it lap at her palm.

"We knew some things about that man," Polly began, taking a glimpse at the spot where he died. "He often walked through here with those tours of his. What a rude old fellow he was. I overheard him one time saying lies about Ulysses Meyers over there!" She pointed towards the man's gravestone. "Said he once burned down a building by tossing a cigarette butt into the property. Hah!"

"How nasty," Dolly added. "He was lucky that we didn't catch him saying a lie about one of us. I would have pulled on his ear during his tour and made sure he ate those words."

"He passed on quickly," Cyrus noted. "That explains why he hasn't appeared in *The Yews*." The ghosts and Reva knew that it took spirits a while to cross over from life to death. In fact, Reva's inn had been founded to give "new" spirits a place to rest up as they prepared themselves to cross into the next, eternal phase of existence. The process wasn't instantaneous for anyone.

"It would have made my life much easier if his spirit could come and tell us the truth about what happened that night," Reva admitted, massaging at her tense shoulder. "All we know for certain is that someone who knows how to use a

84

bow and arrow managed to kill him. The only problem is that I don't know who might shoot arrows as a hobby."

"Well, Dolly and I have heard rumors about a young girl that hunts in Shadow Woods with a bow. She might be the one you're looking for," Polly offered, turning around to take a good look at the large evergreens that covered their horizon. The afternoon sun and blue skies contrasted nicely with those pretty green leaves. "She's around your age, Reva. More or less."

"Do you know her name?" Reva perked up, wondering if this was the same girl Brenda mentioned. "Any details about her?"

Dolly and Polly exchanged looks. Then, Polly shrugged.

"We haven't seen this girl in action personally. We've just heard that she can use a bow. Maybe she thought Burton was a deer and shot him by accident."

"Or a hog," Dolly added, snorting underneath her palm. "Oops. That was mean-spirited of me. He treated our cemetery badly, so I guess it's deserved."

"Understandable," Cyrus chimed in. "Based on what I've heard, he didn't have the best personality."

While Cyrus chatted up the twins, Reva stared off into the forests that surrounded *The Yews*. Burton's ex was an archer. Was she the same person hunting in the woods?

...Was she the one responsible for the arrow in his heart?

Chapter 13

The next morning, Reva woke up to an odd tapping sensation on her legs. She ignored it at first, the lulls of sleep too powerful to break away from.

Then, the tapping turned into a gentle scratch. Again, she didn't feel like checking on that.

Finally, a small weight planted itself firmly on her chest.

"Reva!"

She jolted, opening her eyes to see Pistol seated on her. He glared down at her with slits for pupils, tail wagging violently behind his little body.

"I've been trying to wake you up for ages now! Are you trying to ignore me or something?"

"Pistol…" Reva started, holding up a hand. She then began rubbing at her tired eyes. "I'm sleeping. I don't want to hear it."

"But this is *important*!" The familiar dug his paw into her chest. "Get up right now, it's an emergency. What if the building was burning down? What if someone else got killed in front of the inn? Reva, answer me before I start tearing up your bedroom."

She cracked open one of her eyes.

"Are either one of those things happening?"

"Nope." Pistol shook his head. "But they could have been, and it could have been too late to act now, everyone would already be dead."

"What's the emergency, Pistol?" Reva yawned, snuggling into her pillow. "Make it quick or else I'm going back to bed."

"Cyrus and I keep smelling something strange in one of the hallways. I tried to walk past it earlier and I almost vomited everywhere. It was nasty, but I can't really pinpoint what the smell was."

Finally, Pistol said something worthy of her attention. She sat up in bed, reaching over for a discarded cardigan that she kept near her bedside. She tugged it on, keeping on her pajamas underneath.

"Thank you! You're finally ready to take some action!" Pistol chastised, following her out of the room. "If you waited any longer, I was going to make Cyrus crawl in that ventilation shaft and dig out whatever's stinking up the place."

"How dare you insinuate that I should do such degrading physical labor!" Cyrus asked, overhearing them as they ascended the stairway to the second floor. "My apologies, Reva. We didn't mean to wake you up that early."

87

"Who's we?" Pistol challenged. "I definitely meant to."

"Ignore him, he hasn't been fed his morning kibble yet. That explains why he's so ferocious." Cyrus led the way towards the faulty ventilation shaft in question.

Taking a few steps in that direction, Reva immediately understood why they were complaining so heavily about the smell. She gagged, quickly covering her nose and mouth at the odor. She swallowed hard, feeling some bile already rising in her throat.

"What... *is* that?" Reva managed out, coughing a few times. "I don't think my inn has ever smelled that bad!"

"See?" Pistol said, in a matter-of-fact tone. "That's what you get for ignoring me."

"Shush, Pistol, you tend to act overdramatic on purpose, so I was calling your bluff."

"And I wasn't bluffing," the familiar continued, prancing around in the hallway with a confident pep. "Now, hurry up and fix the ventilation shaft before I take my anger out on the next person I see."

"Don't attack our paying customers!" Cyrus exclaimed. "Our mortals! That's highly rude and immoral of you. They have nothing to do with this situation. In fact, I'd say they are victims just as much as we are."

"This stench is physically assaulting me and my nose right now. *It's* immoral." The cat said.

"Alright." Reva held her hands up, hoping for peace between the two. "Has anyone else complained about this smell, Cyrus?"

"Just about everyone who resides in the rooms of this hallway, I believe." Cyrus grimaced, leaning on the wall. "I think we should make it up to them somehow. Complimentary snacks later, perhaps? Maybe even a discount if they stay a couple more nights?"

"We're not a charity organization, silly, we have a business to run," Pistol said. "We can't afford unnecessary losses in revenue. Plus, what if this shaft is really broken? Then we have to cave in and start spending some cash to fix the dumb thing."

"I didn't know you were my personal assistant and bookkeeper, Pistol," Reva quipped, tossing him a quick grin. "What else? Can you be my lawyer, too?"

"You'll have to pay me for my services at that point. I'm only one cat and you're starting to stretch me a little thin."

"I need a ladder," Reva announced, staring up at the ventilation shaft attached to the hallway's ceiling. She was a few feet short of reaching it. "Do you know where I put that old thing, Cyrus?"

"I'll get that for you right now," Cyrus reassured, dashing off down the stairs and into one of their storage rooms besides the kitchen. He came back with the metal object underneath one of his arms. "Please be careful with this contraption, Reva. I don't want you hurting yourself over this."

Reva felt impressed. It took ghosts a while to learn how to handle three-dimensional objects with their spirit bodies. Cyrus had honed his skills.

"It's a two-step ladder, dummy. If she manages to hurt herself on that, I'll be impressed," Pistol said, earning a scoff and rolled eyes from Reva and Cyrus for his comment. "Why are you two treating me so badly? I'm right!"

Taking the ladder from Cyrus, Reva positioned it steadily underneath the shaft. In just two steps, she was eye-level with the ventilation tunnel. Grabbing its cover, she hauled it open to inspect what was inside.

Wow, I wish I didn't have eyes, Reva thought bitterly to herself.

In the middle of the ventilation tunnel, she spotted a dead serpent, festering silently as its odor stunk up *The Dimidio Inn.* Whoever killed the poor creatures slit it from its lower jaw halfway down its body.

What horrified her the most was the eerie message written in red across the side of the tunnel. *The snake must die,* it read. She assumed the perpetrator used the snake's blood to write the text, considering some red droplets oozed down the bottoms of the letters.

"Reva?" Cyrus asked, jolting her out of her daze. "What do you see? Is it anything grave?"

"Can you, uh…" Reva tried her best not to vomit. "Get me some gloves, please? Now?"

"On it."

Pistol stayed behind, watching with wide eyes as Cyrus returned from the kitchen downstairs, handing over a pair of latex gloves that Reva hastily pulled on. Then, taking a deep breath before doing so, she reached over to grab by its head and tail. Carefully, she tried not to let the mess get any larger.

She was also trying not to spill out her *own* stomach contents by handling the serpent.

Cyrus and Pistol recoiled in horror as they caught sight of the dead snake, with the familiar darting a few paces away before whipping around and staring back in horror.

"What is that thing, Reva?!" Pistol demanded. "How did it even get up there?!"

"How am I supposed to know?" Reva grimaced, accepting Cyrus' silent offer to take the serpent from her hands and dispose of it himself. "I don't know what to do about this. I mean, do I call the police? I've never experienced this."

"Absolutely not, they're going to think we're crazier than we already are!" Pistol neared closer, seeing that Cyrus already disappeared with the snake. "Let's just be quiet about it now that we've removed it. Get some air freshener in this hallway, spritz it a few times, and we'll be good to go. No one has to know!"

Thinking about the menacing message she'd seen in the ventilation shaft, she wondered if it was worth worrying about. The serpent's death was symbolic somehow, but its meaning was passing over her head. She didn't understand who or what the snake was supposed to represent.

She wasn't sure she wanted to find out.

"Reva?" The familiar stared up at her, batting at her toes. "You're still with me, right? You look a little shell-shocked and, don't worry, I am, too."

"Gee, thanks so much for your words of encouragement, Pistol," she replied, gathering up the ladder and taking it downstairs. Using her magic, she flipped the cover of the ventilation shaft so that it covered the tunnel once more. "I need a shower."

"And I need some soup!" Pistol raced down the stairs. "Man, I'm starving."

The more she thought about it, the more her breathing quickened. Who left that serpent behind? They wanted to leave a message, and even though she couldn't decipher it, they'd succeeded in making her blood run cold.

Why was this happening to her *now*?

Chapter 14

Reva spent the rest of the morning on high alert. It didn't help that her aunt wasn't returning any of her calls, no matter how many times she tried to contact her. With her hands trembling, she dialed her aunt's number once again and waited for a response.

Ten times. She tried calling her aunt *ten* times, but none of them went through. Slamming her palm against the kitchen island, Reva paced around before she decided what she wanted to do next. Pocketing her phone, she planned on checking up on her aunt in person. She couldn't stand not hearing from her, since her mind tricked her into thinking the worst possible thing happened.

Just as she made her way out the kitchen, she stopped dead in her tracks halfway across the lobby. Entering slowly with a small smile on her face, Aunt Alva crossed the hotel lobby carrying a small grocery bag.

"There you are, dear." Alva held the bag up for her. "Mind carrying these to the kitchen? I plan on experimenting with a new recipe soon."

"Aunt Alva," Reva breathed out, hurrying over and taking the bag from her hands. "Why weren't you answering any of my calls? I was worried! I thought something happened to you!"

"Don't be silly, my darling. This is Shadow Woods. Nothing bad can happen to me here."

Reva scoffed, helping her aunt to the kitchen by linking her arm with hers.

"Yeah. That was before a detective came into town and started accusing you of murder," she replied, hauling the groceries up on the kitchen island. "What happened with your interrogation? I tried asking that stubborn jerk when I bumped into him at *Terror Tales* but he wasn't helpful at all."

"I've got some bad news, Reva," Alva admitted, placing a hand over her niece's forearm and squeezing tightly. "That detective seems to think I have something to do with Burton's death."

Reva's mouth fell ajar. Slowly, her fists balled up and anger pooled in the darkness of her eyes. Aunt Alva could recognize the fury brewing up in her heart, so she forced her hand into one of Reva's fists.

"Don't worry. You didn't let me explain the whole thing."

"What more is there to explain, Auntie?" Reva asked, exasperated. "He's accusing you of *murder* when he doesn't have evidence to prove it! What kind of detective is he? Did he *buy* his way through training?"

"Reva, please." Alva patted her hand, trying to get her to calm down. "Listen to me. I explained the situation to Detective Carver. Unfortunately, I had to tell him the truth about my relationship with Burton Crabb."

"Relationship?" Reva recoiled. "What do you mean?"

"Well, it wasn't a nice one. I had a few fights with the man here and there because of those ridiculous ghost tours he often used to parade through *The Yews*. I'm sure you know the ones I'm talking about."

"Of course."

"I told the detective that I didn't like the way Burton allowed his guests to litter and soil the cemetery that we spend so much time cleaning," she continued. "That explains why I left those signs for him near the entrance. I wanted to keep him out for good reason. Apparently, in the detective's eyes, this makes me a person of interest in the investigation."

That idiot, Reva thought to herself. Instead, she trailed her tongue over her teeth and sighed. She held back all the words she wanted to say about him. It would distress her poor aunt.

"He also took samples of my fingerprints to see if they matched with the ones they found at the crime scene. They didn't have any previous samples of them because I wasn't registered in their police database. Now I am."

"Aunt Alva..." Reva shook her head, pulling away from her aunt's grasp. "You're too calm about this. You just let him do this to you and you're not *mad* about it?"

"What's there to be angry about, dear?" Aunt Alva rested a hand on her hip. "I wasn't the one responsible, so I don't have anything to worry about."

"Exactly!" Reva exclaimed. "You didn't have anything to do with this case, and yet, he's still taking your fingerprint samples and interrogating you as if you did!"

"Honestly, my love, I don't think it's that big of a deal. Once he realizes that I didn't kill him, everything will be fine. You're worrying too much about this."

"No. He's going to take this as an opportunity to frame you. I can already tell." Reva stormed out of the kitchen towards the hotel's entrance. "He's going to hear from me, I promise you–"

"Reva!" Aunt Alva stood in the kitchen's doorway, sending her a concerned look. "What are you about to do? For your sake and mine, I hope you're not about to start trouble in the police department over this."

"Auntie, please." Reva turned around slowly, her arms dropping limply to her sides. "I need to talk to him about the way he's handling the case. I don't think he's doing a good job."

"I wouldn't do that." Alva stepped forward, crossing her arms over her chest. She leaned with a shoulder against the wall. "You're just walking right into his headquarters, you know. Where he has the most power. One step out of line and he can use that against you."

"I'll be careful with my word choice and my actions to avoid something like that."

"Really? I know you." Alva smiled wide. "You don't do either of those things when you're in the heat of an argument."

"I..." Reva didn't like getting put on the spot like that. When she was a teenager, Aunt Alva used to do that all the time. She didn't appreciate it then, certainly not as an adult, either. "I would behave. I just want to tell him what's on my mind and why he should stop bothering you. That's all."

"Honey, I know you already formed these notions in your mind about the man based on your first impression of him, but I'm asking you to reconsider them."

Swallowing thickly, Reva recognized the sincerity behind her aunt's words. She *meant* that.

"Based on what I've seen from him so far, he seems like an intelligent, hard-working young man who wants to make a good impression on the town by taking on his first murder case. He's working diligently to get things right and I assume that he's going to work hard at finding the truth."

"How did you manage to deduce all this about him already?" Reva pressed, narrowing her eyes. "I'm thinking the exact opposite. I think he's sloppy, unprofessional, and rude. He's arrogant and full of himself. Auntie, I'm sure you wouldn't be saying all these things if you saw the way he came in here a few days ago to tell me about Burton's murder!"

"I don't doubt you," Alva assured. "However, I was fortunate to see a side of that young man that commands respect. He didn't treat me badly when I was at the police station. On the contrary, he apologized often for how the situation inconvenienced me and how he wants to stay in touch to just check up on how I'm doing."

Reva scoffed. That didn't sound like the Matt Carver she met. Absolutely not.

"Your perception of him is biased right now and that's alright. I just hope that you can see the young man in a

98

more positive light sometime in the future. I promise you that he's not as bad as you think."

"I don't know, Auntie," she admitted. "Our personalities don't mix very well. Oil and water. We just don't work well."

"Why's that?"

Reva shrugged. "Sometimes, the things he says annoy me. Likewise, I'm pretty sure he can say the same thing about me. I don't think I'll ever see the guy in a positive light."

"I'm sure your opinions will change eventually. After all, our attitudes don't remain static. We're ever-changing beings with a world of potential at our fingertips. Don't ever forget that."

"I got it, Auntie. Thank you." That being said, she turned back towards the entrance to leave.

Aunt Alva called out again. "Re–"

"I'm just heading off to the store. We need some more toiletries since we're running out. Don't worry." Tossing a glance over her shoulder, she smiled. "I'm not going to bug that detective anymore."

With that, Alva calmed down.

"Thank you, my dear. I'll see you later, then."

Waving goodbye, Reva made her way towards her Jeep and turned it on. Toiletries could wait. She had a detective that she wanted to straighten out.

Chapter 15

The front desk receptionist of the Shadow Woods Police Department typed away at her computer as she pressed a telephone between her shoulder and ear. The person on the other end of the line spoke loudly, causing the young woman to wince occasionally and botch the details she hastily inputted into the computer.

"T-Thank you, sir, we'll start looking into your request soon. I'll transfer these details to one of my superiors."

Sighing deeply, she placed the phone back into its hold on the desk. She didn't get a chance to compose herself after the call since Reva awaited her attention impatiently, tapping her fingers along the counter and smiling tightly once the woman met her gaze.

"Hello," Reva began. "I would like to speak to Detective Matt Carver, please. It's urgent."

"What's the reason for this visit, ma'am? Is it in relation to an investigation or–"

"Yes, it is."

The receptionist paused from typing, glancing up at Reva who continued to fidget at the prospect of waiting any moment longer to confront this man. Clearing her throat, the woman started clicking through the files on her computer. Reva couldn't see what she was doing.

"I'm sorry, ma'am, but Detective Carver is currently in a meeting with someone. If you'd like, you can wait in the lobby until he's free or you can come back another time and check if he's available."

Reva cracked her knuckle. She didn't *want* to come back and she didn't *want* to wait. Although she knew it wasn't the receptionist's fault, Reva still laughed dryly at the suggestion and shook her head.

"I'm afraid I can't do that."

"Excuse me?" The receptionist's back straightened. "Then what do you plan to do?"

"I need to speak with him right now. I'm sorry."

"Ma'am—"

The receptionist stumbled out of her chair as Reva darted down the adjacent hallway. The witch shouldered past officers and interns that walked through the corridor. Reva banked on the fact that the receptionist was so young and so new on the job, she wouldn't know how to handle situations like these, and would feel too afraid to yell out and cause a scene.

"Ma'am!" the receptionist exclaimed in a tight whisper, gently tapping Reva's shoulder as she continued to search for Matt's office. "I need you to return to the front desk, please, because I can't allow you to see Detective Carver at this time."

Finally sighting the office door with the plaque *Detective Matt Carver* on it, Reva quickened her stride. To no surprise, the door was locked. Hiding the knob with her body before the receptionist reached her side, Reva mumbled a spell that discreetly unlocked the handle. Then she opened it abruptly.

Jumping up from his seat, Matt balked at the sight of her. Across from him sat Brenda Braceling, sobbing into a tissue. Reva flinched, unsure of the scene that she walked into. Meanwhile, the receptionist gasped, covering her mouth with a hand.

"Miriam," Matt said, directed towards the receptionist. "Why did you let this woman into my office?"

"I-I tried to stop her, Detective, but she's adamant to talk to you."

"How did you even..." Matt ran a hand through his hair. "I thought I locked that door!"

"Obviously not," Reva deadpanned, shrugging. "I needed to speak to you about the investigation. I'm not leaving until I do."

"Detective," Miriam said, taking a glimpse at Reva. "Should I...?"

"It's alright. You can return to your post. I'll handle things from here."

The bashful woman nodded quickly before hurrying away from the office. Meanwhile, Reva stood firm in his doorway, trading glances with Brenda, who wiped furiously at her eyes with the tissue in her hands.

"What are you doing here?" Matt repeated, gritting his teeth. "I'm sure Miriam told you that I was busy. You had no right to barge into my office like that."

"Well, I wanted to. I need you to leave my aunt out of this investigation. There's no reason for this. She didn't have a motive for killing Burton."

"Are you the one with the case file?" Matt challenged. "Have you been interviewing witnesses and potential suspects? Did you investigate the clues?"

Kind of, she almost said, but that would have blown her cover.

"Your aunt is a suspect in the investigation, just accept it already. I'll do whatever I need to uncover the truth. How many times do I have to repeat this simple information to get it through that head of yours?"

"Detective…" Brenda whispered, looking up. "But you remember what I just told you, right? About–"

"Yes, Miss Braceling, I do. I already took note of what you said, there's no reason to repeat it."

103

"What did she say?" Reva interjected. "Something about the case? Another suspect?"

"She didn't say anything–"

"I was telling him how I think Burton's brother may have…" Brenda trailed off, whimpering slightly. Matt facepalmed midway through her sentence. "His name is Mackie. Mackie Crabb. On the day of Burton's death, I-I saw them fighting outside *Terror Tales*. I didn't know why, but…"

"That's it." Rounding his desk, Matt headed straight for Reva. He grabbed her by the arm, taking her outside of his office and closing the door behind them. "I'm tired of this, I really am."

"So am I."

"If you were, you would understand that I'm only doing my job and I'm trying to do things right. I can't just ignore your aunt when she's a viable suspect in the case!"

"Viable suspect?" Reva repeated incredulously. "You can't be serious. You've already spoken with her! You probably have an idea of what she's like as a person?"

"I do, but that doesn't mean I can go easy on her. It's not fair."

"I'm trying to get you to realize that you need to start focusing on the other suspects already. Have you even interrogated anyone else yet?"

"I'm *getting* to that. Things like this take time."

"You have everything right in front of you!" Reva gestured towards his office. "Don't you realize that Brenda, herself, could be a suspect in this case? And now she's mentioning Burton's brother! He could have been the one behind this, too."

"Reva, I get what you're saying, but–"

"There's also another suspect! Burton's ex-girlfriend or ex-flame or whatever she was. *She* knew how to work a bow and arrow. Apparently, she often hunts in the Shadow Woods forest. Have you even looked into her yet?"

"Hold on a second, how…" A pensive frown appeared on his face. "How do you know about all this? What ex-flame? Brenda admitted that she had a relationship with Burton, so she's the only former partner I know of."

"You're not the only one who's been doing some research," Reva replied. "I want this case to be solved as much as you do. That's why I've been trying to help out as best as I can."

"You shouldn't," he maintained. "You're a civilian. This isn't your business to meddle with."

"Keep saying that all you want; it's not going to stop me. I just want my aunt's name cleared from this situation. She told me that you took her fingerprints. Did you place her in whatever database you have?"

"No, of course not, because she wasn't booked," Matt shot back. "I only wanted them as a reference to the fingerprints we collected from Burton's body. I have some people analyzing them in a lab not far from here, they're going to get back to me if they find a match or not."

"Sounds like a waste of time to me. My aunt didn't do anything."

"We'll see what science says about it."

"Forget about that!" Reva exclaimed. "When it comes to things like this, you can *feel* it. In here." She pointed at her heart. "It's an intuitive feeling."

"I don't believe in that sort of stuff."

"You should. My aunt can't even work a bow and arrow. How would she be able to shoot someone cleanly through the heart, in that case? Highly unlikely if you consider things rationally."

"See, I want to trust that you're telling me the truth, but I can't. There's a chance you're covering for her, which I'd understand since you obviously love her very much to go through these lengths." Matt sighed, pinching the bridge of his nose. "Please. Stay out of the investigation from now on."

"I will if you leave my aunt alone."

"Reva." Chuckling low, Matt laughed through his frustration. "You already know that I can't do that."

106

"Then I'm going to keep popping up until we figure this one out," she promised.

Chapter 16

"I'm thoroughly disturbed."

"You're still talking about the snake, Pistol?" Reva asked, leaning on the counter of *The Dimidio Inn.* After her brief visit to the Shadow Woods Police Department, she headed straight home to find Cyrus and Pistol in the lobby. Her aunt cooked dinner in the kitchen. "You're not the one who had to haul it out of here."

"Does it look like I have the opposable thumbs needed to do such a thing?" The familiar held out his paws for good measure.

"You have a jaw," Cyrus pointed out.

"I wasn't going to pick up that stinky snake with my teeth. You're sick for even suggesting that."

"I'm just glad that we don't have to smell that thing anymore," Reva said, glancing up towards the second-floor hallway where they found the festering creature. "Do you two have any idea how long it might have been up there?"

"No clue, but we had received complaints about a strange smell for quite some time now," Cyrus replied, taking a step closer towards Reva. "Thank you for checking the ventilation shaft, Reva. Without you, the hotel wouldn't be the same."

Pistol dry-heaved. Reva smiled, patting Cyrus on the shoulder. The small action made him beam.

"Thanks. I have to go in and clean the shaft later. I can't leave some snake residue behind in there." And the blood. She refused to talk about that aloud. "I also want to figure out who left the snake there in the first place, but that's a can of worms that I'm not prepared to deal with right now."

"Why not?" Pistol perked up. "Just leave it to me! I'll teach them a lesson about leaving random animals around our hotel like that. They'll regret it."

"Bud, they can just pick you up by the scruff and immobilize you." Reva demonstrated by doing so, which made Pistol fall limp under her grasp. "See?"

"Let go of me," Pistol demanded, still frozen. "Stop airing my weaknesses like that."

Dropping him back on the counter, Pistol swatted her hand away and furiously licked at his fur.

"Reva, I wanted to ask you if you were free later," Cyrus began, straightening out his clothes.

"Today? I'm feeling kind of gross," she said, glancing down at her outfit. Wrinkled and somewhat dirtied by her adventurous day. "I want to shower."

"You look perfectly radiant to me. As always. You match the sun's rays with your brilliance."

"Gross!" Pistol spat. "What's with all this lovesick nonsense you're letting loose in front of me? Are you not ashamed of yourself?"

"Pistol, be nice," Reva scolded gently.

"I wanted to recite a poem to you," Cyrus admitted. "I've worked on it for quite some time and would like some feedback. Of course, I must admit that I used you as my muse."

"Ew!" Pistol continued, earning him a rough rub on the head from Reva. He hissed. "Don't ruin my fur again!"

"Well, stop being mean."

"I'm not!" Pistol sauntered over to Cyrus, standing on his toes to appear somewhat taller than he already was. Being a small kitten meant he lacked in the height department, unfortunately. "She's going to be too busy to hear your love poems, Mister."

"Busy doing what?" Reva asked, knitting her brows together.

"Um... hello? Cleaning out my litter box and feeding me tuna? Did you forget about all your obligations and responsibilities because someone offered to read a poem to you?"

"You're too funny," she replied, enjoying the way Pistol took a victory lap around the counter. "I'll think about it, Cyrus, because that sounds like a great–"

Suddenly, her sentence got cut short by a clamor coming from the kitchen. It sounded like metal pots and pans falling to the ground. Reva's eyes widened, hurrying over since she knew her aunt was the only one in the kitchen.

"Aunt Alva?" Reva called out, entering the kitchen. She gasped, seeing her aunt collapsed on the floor. "Auntie!"

"Oh, my." Cyrus hurried, gathering the things Alva accidentally pushed to the floor when she fell. "Alva, are you alright? Please don't tell me you overworked yourself. I can take over for dinner if you'd like."

"Auntie, what happened?" Reva asked, brushing the gray hairs out of her face and cupping her cheeks. "Did you hit your head? Did someone attack you?"

"Reva…" Alva swallowed hard, hoping to bring some moisture to her dry mouth. "Water, please…"

"I'll get it," Cyrus offered, already bustling around to fetch her a fresh cup.

Pistol sniffed the air, taking a long whiff. His tail curled upwards towards the ceiling as he glanced around the kitchen. The small gray hairs on his body shot straight outwards.

"Something's wrong," he commented low, continuing to stare around at the relatively empty kitchen. "It doesn't feel right."

"I felt my energy drain," Alva whispered, after taking a long gulp of water from the cup Cyrus provided her. "It happened so suddenly that I didn't have time to brace myself."

"Auntie..." Reva's heart dropped. "That only ever happens to you when a malevolent presence is nearby. It sucks your energy away."

"No wonder she collapsed," Pistol said, turning towards them. "I'm feeling that malicious energy, too."

Reva raised a hand to her mouth, her fingers trembling violently. Evil vibes? Were they somehow related to the serpent in the ventilation shaft? Something sinister lingered around her hotel, but she couldn't comprehend what. Aunt Alva groaned, reaching for the nearest counter to tug herself up. Reva and Cyrus helped her, guiding her by the hands.

"Thank you for the help, but I'm feeling a little better."

"You're not going to work on anything else for the rest of the day," Reva demanded. "My orders. I can't have you hurting yourself."

"You shouldn't worry about me, Reva. Really." Aunt Alva smiled, though the action lacked strength. Reva nearly started crying. "I can go home and read some books. Maybe even brew some tea–"

Glass shattered loudly in another room, causing everyone to flinch and duck to the floor. Reva instinctively covered Aunt Alva's body with her own, whipping around to try and find the source of the sound. Cyrus scrambled out the door to investigate. Meanwhile, Alva grabbed at her wrist.

"Reva–"

"Auntie, stay here with Pistol." Reva kissed her on the temple, running a hand through her aunt's hair. "Cyrus and I will find out what happened."

"Please be careful, my dear," Alva breathed out, her eyes fluttering closed as she sat upon the ground and leaned her head against the drawer.

"Alva, stay with me," Pistol demanded. He stared at Reva. "Go! What if it's a break-in?"

"I-I…" Reva scrambled to her feet, already heading out the door. "Stay here!"

Rushing out of the hotel, she turned right when she heard Cyrus call out for her name. She rounded the building, expecting the worst. Beside one of the windows, they saw a masked individual with a rock in their hands. When they saw Reva coming, they dropped the rock and started to sprint in the other direction.

Clenching her jaw, Reva lifted a hand up towards the vandal. Uttering a spell, she created a wide forcefield in front of the fleeing form. They ran straight into the barrier, with the impact knocking them backwards a few feet. Yowling in pain, the individual writhed on the ground and gripped at their abdomen.

Cyrus sighed, rubbing at her shoulder.

"Good work on that, beloved."

She nodded. Then, she gestured towards the individual's ankles. Cyrus understood immediately, heading over to pin the person down.

Taking advantage of the fact that the individual was still disoriented, Reva mumbled another spell. A small rope materialized in her palms, which she intended to use to pin the person's hands behind their back if things escalated.

She stood over the individual, who started sobbing. Crouching beside the figure, Reva tried to make sense of everything that happened. First, her aunt collapsed on the kitchen floor and warned of a malevolent presence in their midst. Then, someone threw a rock through one of her hotel windows. Was everything connected somehow? She just couldn't understand.

"Who are you?" Reva demanded, shaking the person's shoulder. She still couldn't see their face completely due to the ski mask, but she noticed tears brimming in blue eyes. "Why did you just throw a rock through one of my hotel windows?"

"I-I..." It was the voice of a young boy. Reva shared a wide-eyed look with Cyrus. "I... I was told I had to!"

Reva's breath hitched in her throat. What was happening to her hotel?

Chapter 17

"What does he mean by that, Reva?"

Rage and confusion bubbled deep in her chest. At the same time, pity accumulated steadily in her heart for the young boy who started sobbing on the ground. Peeling the ski mask from his face, Reva caught a good look at his face.

Just a kid.

"Tell me everything that you know," she ordered softly, helping the whimpering boy up into a seated position. "If you do, I promise I won't call the police for what you just did."

"P-Please don't," the boy pleaded, shaking his head. "I-I don't want to get in trouble... I just wanted the money so that I could help my family out. My dad just lost his job."

Letting out a shaky sigh, Reva subtly motioned to Cyrus. On cue, the ghost loosened his hold on the boy's ankles. She placed a hand on his shoulder, comforting him as he hunched over with soft sobs.

"What's your name?" Reva asked, after giving the boy enough time to compose himself.

He wiped away at his face, hiccupping through his words.

"Paul."

"Who paid you to do this, Paul? Who told you to come to my hotel and break my windows to teach me a lesson?"

"I… I was walking near the town square yesterday and this woman came up to me. I don't remember her name very well, but she had curly blonde hair."

Reva stiffened.

"Plus, she wore these big sunglasses that covered most of her face so I couldn't see her eyes."

"Donna Corona."

"T-That's it," the boy affirmed, sniffling. "That's her name. She asked me if I wanted to make some easy money. At first, I thought she was just scamming me or something, but she said that I need to vandalize your hotel. If I did, she would give me five hundred dollars in cash."

Fiddling with his thumbs, the boy averted his gaze.

"She already gave me the first half of the money. Ma'am." His eyes met with hers, bloodshot and still brimming with tears. "I'm sorry that I did this to your property. I didn't make the right choice; I understand that now."

"Do you have any other affiliation with Donna?" Reva asked. "Have you done jobs like this for her in the past?"

115

"No, ma'am, no." The boy adamantly shook his head. "Yesterday was the first day I even met her. Before that, I had never seen her before. She doesn't look like she's a part of this town, anyway. She looks… richer."

"Snobbier, too," she quipped, under her breath. "I get it, though. You were just trying to help your family. I understand."

"...Really?" The boy's eyes went big, seeing that Reva didn't respond to him with anger. "You're not going to call the police or anything?"

"No, but I want you to take this as a lesson." Grabbing the boy by the shoulder, she made sure he looked her directly in the eyes as she said her next words. "Don't go around accepting money from random strangers in exchange for illegal tasks. You might not get so lucky the next time you choose to do something like this."

"Believe me, ma'am, I'm never going to do something like this ever again. Never."

"That's comforting to hear. We don't need more trouble running around the town. One person is enough."

"Are you referring to the woman?"

"Absolutely."

Helping the boy to his feet, Reva brushed off the grass and dirt that gathered upon his clothes once the forcefield sent him flying.

116

"Go back home," she advised. "And when you see Donna Corona again, because I'm sure you will, tell her that you finished the job so that you can get the other half of that money."

"Ma'am, but..." The boy hesitated. "That doesn't feel right..."

"Your family needs it, right?"

Slowly, he nodded.

"Then go for it. Don't worry about it."

"But–"

"Just listen to what I'm saying, kid. Go." Reva waved him off with a hand.

The boy didn't fight about it. Turning around, he quickly sped off towards the front of the inn, where he cut a sharp left and started running towards the direction of town square. Staring after him, Reva stayed silent until a gentle hum interrupted her thoughts. She turned, seeing Cyrus gaze at her with a soft smile and a slight twinkle in his eyes.

"That's very admirable, what you just did."

She shrugged. "I didn't want to be too difficult with him. He's a kid who made a dumb mistake. We all went through that at one point or another."

"Of course, but he threw a rock through your window in pursuit of some monetary acquisition. Even still, you showed him mercy. Not many people have the strength to do that."

"...Whatever." Reva shook her head, returning to the spot where the vandalism took place. She grimaced. "He really did a number on my building."

"Indeed. What if he planned on striking more of your windows? Would you have forgiven him, then?"

"I'm not sure. I'm not even thinking about that right now," she admitted, careful to not step on the glass shards that littered the grass beneath them. "I can't believe she was willing to do that. Hiring *children* to do her dirty work? She must be sick in the head."

"Or she's been so pampered her entire life that she doesn't recognize the nonsense behind her actions. She's quite silly, I'm afraid."

"I think she knows what she's doing, Cyrus. She just doesn't care about hurting others to get what she wants."

Channeling her magic through a spell that Aunt Alva taught her, Reva gathered the small shards and caused them to levitate upwards towards the broken window. Gradually, the pieces came together, one by one, and returned to their original locations in the frame. The spell helped adhere the broken shards back together.

Once she finished, Cyrus let out an impressed sigh.

"You're exceptional at what you do, beloved."

118

"Thanks." Resting her hands on her hips, she gazed at her handiwork. "Good as new, I think." She pressed on the glass, searching for any weak spots. "Yeah. I did a pretty good job."

"I don't think I've known another spellcaster as talented and clever as you are." Cyrus kept his hands behind his back, standing a little taller as he showered Reva with compliments. "I've known many who cannot memorize as many spells as you do. Others do not have the finesse needed to complete the complicated spells that you achieve with ease."

"I had a great teacher growing up, you know," Reva replied. "It wasn't all me. Auntie Alva helped me every step along the way, so everything I know now is because of her."

"You Brennans are a spectacular bunch."

"Thank you," she said, her smile faltering as she thought back on her parents. "I just hope I can make my family proud."

"What do you mean? Of course, you will!" Cyrus furrowed his eyebrows together in confusion. "In fact, you already have. I'm sure your ancestors are all gleaming with pride, seeing the person you've become."

"You're too nice to me, Cyrus. Sometimes, I wonder what I did to deserve someone like you."

"It's nothing," he responded softly. A comment like that would have made his human self flush. "I hope you don't underestimate your worth, my beloved. You deserve the world and more."

Laughing, she patted him on the arm. "You're a great friend, you know."

The gesture, although well-intentioned, caused his ego to deflate. He swallowed thickly, following after her as she continued towards *The Dimidio Inn*, intending to enter the building.

"Reva, I…"

She turned around, waiting for his next words.

"I… am glad that we have a close relationship. I hope we can continue being as close as we are for the foreseeable future."

"I do, too." Reva leaned on the entrance of the hotel. "Many people don't have close friends that they can rely on, so I'm happy that you and I have that bond. Are you coming inside? I want to check on Auntie Alva and see how she's been holding up since her fall."

"No, I'm going to head to *The Yews* and clear my head a bit." Cyrus gestured towards the nearby cemetery. "I hope that isn't an issue."

"Not at all. Go have fun."

As she entered the hotel, Cyrus watched her leave. His shoulders hunched over and he pinched at the bridge of his nose, sighing deeply as he began his short, but purposely gradual, journey towards the graveyard.

"What a fool am I?" Cyrus muttered to himself. "A great friend. Is that how she sees me?"

Chapter 18

Pouring more tea for her aunt, Reva handed over the small porcelain cup. They sat in the kitchen, where her aunt took the chair by the window while she stood beside the counter. Setting aside the kettle, she gazed at her aunt.

"I hope you're feeling better, Auntie."

"Much better, my love. Thank you." Aunt Alva took a long sip of tea, cherishing the taste of lavender on her tongue. "What happened to the individual outside? Did you let him go?"

"Yeah. I didn't feel like reporting the incident or anything like that."

"He broke one of your windows, Reva. Vandalized your property! In situations like these, a police report is absolutely warranted."

"He's just a kid, Auntie. It doesn't sit right with me," she admitted gently, staring down at her shoes. "Donna Corona probably coerced him into doing her dirty work while

121

she could sit back and laugh about the whole thing. She's slimy."

"Are you sure you don't want to talk to the police about it?" Aunt Alva pressed. "There's no shame in doing so."

Reva thought, picking at the calloused patch on her left palm. Spellcasting could do a number on her body sometimes.

"If I report this to the police, I think I'd have to talk to that detective again," she admitted. "I don't want to go through that. Not right now."

"So, you're just planning to avoid him for the time being? That's not viable."

Shrugging, Reva didn't want to speak to him or about him. She quickly changed their conversation.

"Auntie, I'm starting to wonder if everything that has happened in the hotel is connected somehow. These events are simultaneous, which is making me think that a single person or entity is behind everything." Reva sighed, digging her hands into the counter's edge. "Probably Donna."

"What else has happened?" Aunt Alva set aside her teacup. "Besides the boy who just broke your window."

"We also found a dead snake in one of the ventilation shafts. It's an intimidation tactic, I'm sure of it. I just can't imagine anyone besides Donna who wants to see me go down. Maybe the detective, too."

"I doubt that one. He doesn't seem like he has the time to dilly-dally like that."

"We can't know for sure. We barely know the guy." Rubbing her clammy hands on her jeans, Reva straightened up. "I'm so confused. Now I have this malevolent energy pervading the hotel that you and Pistol picked up on. I didn't want to believe it but…" She cast a sad glance towards her aunt. "It's all too real to ignore."

"My dear, I haven't felt an energetic presence as strong as that in a very long time. Whatever that was…" Aunt Alva shuddered. "It shouldn't be here."

"Is it a spirit?"

"I can't tell for sure. I hope it's not a demon. Those are difficult to get rid of."

"A demon in our hotel?" Reva rubbed her eyes. "That's just what we need."

"On second thoughts, demons are also accompanied by the scent of rotting flesh and the possession of mortals, who start to act strangely almost immediately. We haven't experienced either one of those things in the hotel, so that's a good sign."

"What if the malevolent energy is Donna Corona?" Reva offered, glancing at her aunt for confirmation. "I mean, she's vile. Evil. The only thing she cares about is herself, her image, and money. Souls like that are rotten."

123

"My dear, it's certainly possible, especially since that young man you caught connects back with that woman. However, I still think it's strange. Even if the woman *was* the culprit behind this, I don't understand how her energetic drain could be so potent."

Reva tilted her head curiously. "What do you mean by that?"

"She's a mortal, isn't she?"

"I...I would *hope* so."

"Maybe we need to do some more digging into her family and background," Aunt Alva suggested. "I'm not convinced a mere mortal could have that much power."

As her aunt made the move to get up, Reva made a sound and guided her back down into her seat. She readjusted the blanket she brought from her bedroom, spreading it across Alva's legs.

"I'm not letting you do any work today. You're done."

"It sounds like you're firing me, my darling."

"I might if you don't listen to me."

"Ooh!" Aunt Alva tapped at her armrest. "You're a ferocious one. But really, love, I'm feeling better. The short break and the tea did me well. Who's going to finish dinner? I was making a special recipe I read in one of my old cookbooks!"

"Hand me the recipe, then. Cyrus and I will finish up the job. I can't guarantee that we will make the food as well as you do, but we'll try our best."

Aunt Alva beckoned her over with a hand. Leaning forward, Reva accepted the kiss on her cheek.

"So where are you heading off to, now?" Aunt Alva asked, watching as she headed towards the door. "You'll make some good use of your time, I hope?"

"I always do!" Reva scoffed. "I wanted to go on a short walk to clear my head. I'll probably stop by *The Yews* while I'm at it and speak with the spirits there. They're much happier without the police invading their space anymore."

"Ah, I heard about that! I also stumbled upon some rumors coming from members of the force. They say that they firmly believe *The Yews* is haunted!" Aunt Alva laughed heartily, holding a hand over her chest. "They're a bit late to that one."

"I'm sure the spirits messed with the officers while they worked. They wouldn't be able to resist."

"I wouldn't put it past them at all." Aunt Alva bowed her head, waving goodbye. "See you later, my dear. And don't forget about my recipe! I'm looking forward to that meal!"

"Got it, Auntie!"

Carefully closing the door, Reva sighed. Despite the tumultuous day, she finally felt herself beginning to calm

125

down. However, the poor boy that she caught still lingered heavily on her mind.

That incident was making her think that Donna was willing to break all ethical and moral codes in order to get what she wanted. That wasn't a surprise, but it made Reva wonder just how far she was willing to go to get *The Dimidio Inn*. Reva planned on fighting back, tooth and nail, regardless of the tactics used against her.

The inn belonged to her mother. Before that, her grandmother, and all of the Brennans through the matriarchal line. If Donna Corona believed that the tradition was going to stop with Reva, the banking heiress was gravely mistaken.

She looked around for any signs of Cyrus and Pistol. She assumed that Cyrus headed towards *The Yews* after they dealt with the vandal. She didn't have a clue where her familiar scrambled off to. He often fell asleep in the wackiest places during the afternoon, so she figured he was in a bush outside somewhere.

Entering the lobby, her mood dropped down a hole when she saw the individual standing in the center of the space. Twirling his shades in his hands, Detective Matt Carver studied the lobby and only stopped when he noticed Reva staring straight at him. While Reva exuded irritation, Matt matched it with indifference. He didn't come to fight.

"Good to see you again, Reva."

126

"What are you doing here?"

"Sheesh. I expected to hear something like 'you too' or 'likewise' but I'm glad we're getting straight to the point." Matt's gaze flickered around in search of something in particular. "Do you know where your aunt is?"

"Why would I tell you that?"

"Because the lab got back to me already and they said that they found her fingerprints on Burton Crabb's clothing. They also found another unidentified individual's print on his jacket, so I need to look into that some more. For now, I would like to speak with Alva once more and question her again about what happened that night."

Feeling her knees buckle at the news, Reva leaned on the nearest wall to avoid falling. It was all too much for one day. She didn't want her aunt to suffer through anything else, but…

"Reva, honey?" A voice called out from the kitchen. "Who are you talking to?"

Closing her eyes, she didn't anticipate her aunt giving out her location so easily. Matt turned towards the voice with an eyebrow perked upwards.

"Don't worry about it, Auntie," Reva replied, somewhat defeated. "I'll handle this."

127

Reva and Matt stood at opposite ends of the lobby. Both had their arms crossed over their chests and equally stubborn looks on their faces.

"My aunt isn't going anywhere with you," Reva said.

"Then I can send out another officer, but we're bringing her in," Matt responded.

"You don't have anything on her," Reva ignored him. "What's a set of fingerprints? I've probably left my fingerprints on your jacket at some point."

"And if I turn up dead, they'll definitely come looking for you."

Reva glared at him.

"What about the other set of prints? Why aren't you trying to find out about them?"

"We are," Matt said, exasperated. "But for now, we need to talk to your aunt. Maybe we can even rule her out as a suspect."

"My aunt isn't well."

"Don't lie to me to try and get out of this," he said wearily. "I've had enough of you trying to interfere with my work."

"I'm not lying," Reva cried. "She fell earlier, she needs to rest."

"What happened?" Matt actually sounded a little concerned. Reva was just surprised that he cared enough to ask. Or pretended to care.

"We don't know," she said. Trying to tell a mortal like Matt about a magical disturbance would only make him more suspicious of her and her family.

"Okay," Matt said sarcastically. "That sounds real worrying. I'll decide if she's well enough to go into the station."

"If she gets worse because of you, I'll make your life so hard, you'll wish you never met me," Reva spat.

"Don't worry," Matt said hotly. "I already do."

He tried to push past her to get to the kitchen, but she refused to budge. He curled his hands into fists and took a deep breath, trying to calm down.

"Look, I'm sorry," he said. "I promise we will take good care of your aunt. We just need to ask her a few questions. This doesn't have to be a big deal."

"You've already talked to her," Reva said. "It's only been a few days, but I can already tell you're pretty bad at your job. You're obsessed with pinning this on my aunt instead of trying to find the real killer."

Matt flushed dark red.

"If she doesn't start giving me some real answers, then I'm going to have to say she is the real killer."

The idea of something happening to Alva made Reva quake with fear and rage. "You're an idiot."

"And you're unbelievable," Matt sputtered. "I'm going to have you arrested."

"For trying to defend my family against your ridiculous accusations?" Reva taunted him. "Good luck with that. I'm the local here. You're just an outsider."

"For obstructing a homicide investigation," Matt said. "I'm serious. If you don't get out of my way, I'm going to take you down to the station first and then come back for your aunt."

Reva noticed the way he was panting, and his hands were shaking at his sides. It was like looking at a volcano about to blow.

"She's not going to want to go with you," she said, hoping that was true. "And don't think you'll get any help from me."

"Once she hears my side of things, I think she will."

Feeling utterly helpless, Reva let Matt slip past her towards the kitchen. When he pushed the door open, Pistol scampered through and skidded on the rug.

"You shouldn't let animals in a kitchen," Matt muttered as the door swung shut again.

"You shouldn't let detectives in kitchens either," Pistol said mockingly. "You okay? That was quite the fight."

Reva turned to look through the round window in the kitchen door. Auntie Alva was still sitting in the chair where they had left her. She had probably heard the whole thing. Reva felt her face get hot with embarrassment, but still didn't regret anything she'd said. A bully like Matt Carver had no business tormenting her family.

"Just doing what I have to do," she said.

"As long as you keep yourself out of trouble," Pistol said.

"I don't go looking for trouble," Reva protested. "Trouble just seems to find me."

Pistol gave her a look that said exactly what he thought of that claim.

"Maybe you should look away from this next part," she told him.

"What does that mean?" Pistol sounded excited. "Are we being bad?"

"I am," Reva muttered.

Making sure she was still visible to the detective in the kitchen, she shifted until she could see out the window into the parking lot. Matt Carver's police cruiser was clearly visible, parked neatly in a space in front of the building. From her spot in the lobby, Reva could see the front tires.

She took a deep breath and centered herself. Even though she was still vibrating with helpless anger, she tried to feed off the energy in her emotions instead of getting lost in the emotions. Power built in her spine and shot down her arms.

It was exhilarating, but not enough for her purposes.

She put aside her anger and thought about her inn and everyone in it. There was Pistol and Cyrus and Auntie Alva. She intended to keep them all safe. The energy of her determination outweighed her anger at Matt Carver.

With a sharp exhale, she sent a powerful burst of magic towards the parking lot. It sped through the walls of the inn and sunk into its intended target, the front tires of Matt's car.

Even from inside the lobby, Reva could see a single, deep slash in each tire. The car slowly sunk as the tires deflated.

"Gotcha," Reva whispered breathlessly, swaying on her feet.

Pistol hopped up on the windowsill to get a better look.

"Nice job," he said. "But keep it together, you don't want to give yourself away."

"I'm okay," Reva said. She could already feel her energy returning like sunlight on a spring day. And she was starving after using that much magic.

She was about to see if there was anything left over from lunch in the kitchen, when Matt and Auntie Alva emerged.

"Thank you for your cooperation, ma'am," Matt was saying.

Reva felt all of her frustration return in an instant, but just then Auntie Alma said innocently, "Is that your car, detective?"

Matt stared past her out into the parking lot. He saw the state of his tires and immediately rounded on Reva.

"What did you do?" he demanded.

"Me?" Reva yelped. "How could I have done anything? I've been here the whole time. Did you see me move from this spot?"

Matt glared at her, clearly trying to piece together how Reva had sabotaged his car.

"Maybe you ran over something on your way in," Auntie Alva offered.

While Matt was still trying to formulate a response, Cyrus slipped back through the wall that faced the cemetery. As usual, he looked upset to see Matt around, but his face quickly brightened when he realized that Matt was not having a good time.

"This looks like fun," he said to Pistol. "I want to play too."

He glided across the room and blew a puff of air into Matt's ear.

The detective let out a strangled yelp and jerked around in a circle, flailing his arms. Reva stifled a burst of laughter.

"Are you alright?" she asked.

"There's something wrong with this place," Matt muttered. "You wait right here."

He pulled the large black walkie-talkie off his belt and held it up to his face.

"This is Detective Carver requesting assistance at the Dimidio Inn."

After a second, a woman dispatcher's voice came crackling through the speaker. "Copy that, Detective. What's the situation?"

"I'm going to need someone to bring another car out here as well as a tow truck. ASAP."

Reva couldn't look at Cyrus or she'd burst out laughing.

"You hit something?" the dispatcher asked.

"No." Matt's face was completely red. "I have a flat tire. Actually, two flat tires."

"Geeze, Carver," the dispatcher sounded amused. "You just got here and you're already damaging police equipment."

"I have a suspect who needs to be interrogated," Matt said stiffly. "Today, if possible."

"Okay, okay, I guess we can get someone out to help you. Wait there."

Matt jammed the walkie-talkie back on his belt and stood fuming. Across the room, Cyrus looked so gleeful, he was practically floating above the floor.

"I don't know how you did this," Matt said. "But I'm going to figure it out."

"Good luck with that," Reva said sweetly.

Chapter 20

"You humans just don't get it," Pistol taunted, walking across the tree branch. "Keeping your balance is pretty easy. See?"

"It's easy when you don't have a lot of mass or width to account for," Reva countered, leaning against the trunk while Cyrus sat by her feet.

That morning, the trio had woken up and headed into the secluded parts of Shadow Woods forest, hoping to find the archer that Dolly and Polly mentioned. Cyrus suggested that they climbed a tree to get a better vantage point. In reality, he probably just wanted an excuse to sit close to Reva for an extended period of time.

135

Pistol sat further down the branch, tucking his arms beneath his body while he gazed at the birds that flew by their heads. Occasionally, he would lick his lips.

Cyrus occupied himself with a book, flicking through the pages and calmly humming a tune that reminded him of his home. Meanwhile, Reva actively searched for the archer, craning her neck in all directions.

In time, she sighed. "Are you two going to help me or what? If I would have known you were just going to sit here and do nothing, I would have come alone."

"My beloved, please don't say that," Cyrus pleaded, shutting his book. "I'll start searching, too."

"I *am* helping. My mere presence should inspire you to get the job done," Pistol replied, batting his tail. He turned around, watching as a hummingbird whizzed by. "Do you think I can catch one of those? Personally, I do. Looks like a piece of cake for a talented kitty like me."

"Pistol, eye on the prize." Reva snapped her fingers. "We need to find the person Dolly and Polly talked about."

"Who are they again? Polly and Holly?" Pistol asked.

"*Dolly*," Cyrus corrected. "You need to start paying more attention to the inhabitants of *The Yews*. They'd appreciate it, you know."

"I think I give them more attention than they deserve." Pistol's whiskers twitched. "Just the other day, I was talking to one of them and they told me that they were a famous sculptor when they were still alive. Pretty cool, but then I asked them to show me their skills with a strange piece of clay I found on the ground, and they refused! They said it wasn't clay, but something else!"

"Poop?" Reva offered. Cyrus chuckled.

"I don't... Well." Pistol mused about that. "You know what? Maybe. However, I still felt unimpressed that he couldn't make something out of it. I mean, it felt malleable."

"You *touched* it?"

"I just batted it around with my paw a little bit. Nothing serious."

"Oh, my." Cyrus massaged at his temples. "I deep-cleaned the carpets in the hallways. I sincerely hope you didn't prance your dirty little paws across them."

"You complained so much about how bad that serpent smelled and now you're playing around with poop," Reva said, shaking her head. "You're unbelievable, Pistol."

"I didn't know what this substance was! Plus, it didn't smell *that* bad. Not compared to the snake."

"I worry about you, sometimes." Cyrus petted his little body, which prompted an abrupt purr from Pistol. "You're so wee but you cause a world of mischief."

"Why, thank you! Someone acknowledges my worth, finally." With his ears twitching in delight, Pistol readjusted

137

his position on the branch so that his arms stretched out in front of him. "I just knew you'd understand."

"I don't think he meant it as a compliment," Reva remarked.

"If he sees it as one, then just let him. He's enjoying himself," murmured Cyrus.

"Reva, stop hating. It's ruining my energy," said Pistol. "When we get back home, can I eat some of that unused salmon from last night's dinner?"

"I'll have to ask Auntie Alva about that."

"Why do we have to ask her?" Pistol scrunched up his nose. "Food is food and it shouldn't go to waste."

"Maybe she wants to use it for another one of her recipes. Dinner last night was her idea, but Cyrus and I took over because I didn't want her working after what happened."

"...Just a little nibble."

"You're misbehaving," Cyrus piped up. "I'll be surprised if Reva caves in and actually gives you what you want."

"She usually does," the cat replied, proudly. "That's one of the perks of being a cat, you know. People give us whatever we want, even when we don't deserve it. It's convenient being cute."

"If only they knew how much of a menace you truly are," Cyrus said.

"Thank you!" Pistol exclaimed. "Cyrus, you truly get me."

"Yeah." Reva nodded. "I should have figured that I wasn't going to get much done by bringing you two along."

"What do you mean?" Cyrus frowned. "I'm helping as much as I can, Reva, but I don't see this individual."

"What if they don't even hunt at this time and we're just waiting around like a bunch of fools?" Pistol asked. "I could have been eating a nice breakfast right now."

"You already did," Reva reminded. "I gave you some special cat milk along with the usual treats you get. You're always spouting nonsense."

"Hey! I do that sometimes, not *all* the time. You're exaggerating."

"Okay." Reva lifted herself off the branch slightly, tightening her grip on the trunk beside her. "I can't hear anything with all this chatter."

"Me neither," Cyrus said.

Mumbling a spell that temporarily amplified her hearing, Reva sucked in a breath and focused on channeling energy toward her ears. Suddenly, all the noises in her vicinity became much more apparent. She could hear leaves from several feet away crackling in the wind, animals scurrying under the foliage, branches creaking from a particularly strong gust.

Then she heard a small twig snap somewhere behind her. She turned around quickly, searching for the origin of the noise. An arrow whizzed straight towards her face.

Reva screamed loudly, dodging out of the way by throwing herself toward the tree trunk. Her abrupt movements caused her balance to falter. Her legs slipped off the branch while her arms clung tightly around it. She dangled there, bark scratching at her skin.

"Reva!" Cyrus exclaimed, scurrying over to support her from falling.

Pistol yowled loudly, claws flicking out, back arching in response to the tumult. He glared towards the woods.

A hooded figure a few yards away stood frozen with a bow in their hands and a bag of arrows around their back. Hissing, Pistol pressed his belly into the branch.

"There's someone over there," he said. "They shot at us!"

"They're probably the person we're looking for!" Reva gasped out, feeling her arms about to give out. Cyrus grabbed at her hand.

"Don't worry, Reva, I'm not going to let you fall."

"They're escaping!" Pistol exclaimed.

The familiar took the initiative, acting quickly to scale down the tree. However, Reva had other plans. Staring down at the fleeing archer, Reva mustered enough magical energy in her body to conduct another spell.

Adrenaline coursed down her right arm and into her fingertips. Her digits curled inward as she raised her arm in an upward motion, which caused the tree roots surrounding the archer to pop out from the ground in an act of brute force. Reva grit her teeth, groaning as she directed the roots to entangle themselves around the archer's feet.

The person stumbled and fell hard on the ground, evident by the sound that reverberated across the forest. Sighing in relief, Reva felt pleased to know that the individual who nearly killed her wasn't going to get away with it.

"Thanks for the help, Cyrus," she whispered, allowing the ghost to support her shaky body as she sat on the tree branch once more. Taking shallow breaths, Reva hugged against the trunk. "I don't think I want to climb up these trees again. Not for a long while."

"I don't blame you, my dear," he replied, brushing her disheveled hair out of her face. "Let's get down there, alright? Take as much time as you need in going down. I can tell that you're jittery."

Nodding, Reva started making her way down. Her nails and fingers clawed into the bark, so she didn't slip as she descended. Cyrus encouraged her, vocalizing his support every step of the way.

Chapter 21

When she finally planted her feet on the ground again, Reva hung onto the trunk for a moment. Her head spun a little bit. With the shock from the situation finally dying down, she gripped at her temple as her heart's pounding subsided.

"Are you alright?" Cyrus asked, placing a hand on her neck.

She nodded, pressing her lips into a thin line. "I am. Thank you for checking up on me. I owe you a lot."

"You don't," he said. "I would do it all again without asking."

Pistol chirped loudly at the assailant, tossing insults at the mortal who couldn't understand a word of what the familiar said.

"Stupid!" Pistol yelled, stomping his paw into the ground. "You're worthless and you're good for nothing! Watch where you're aiming that nasty bow of yours the next time!"

The hooded person continued clawing at the roots that encased their ankles. They heaved, pulling at the gnarled roots more and more desperately, but they didn't budge.

That gave Reva enough time to walk over, crouch beside the archer, and pull off their hood.

142

A blonde-haired woman stared at her with big, brown eyes. Soft freckles dotted her cheeks and nose. When she realized that Reva had her cornered, she yielded and stopped struggling against the roots that trapped her.

"Do you mind telling me why you shot an arrow at my head?"

"I-I didn't mean it at all! Listen." The woman held out her hand. "Please don't do anything to me. I really didn't want to hurt you. I didn't want to hurt anyone, that's never my intention!"

"Then answer my question. Why did you shoot that arrow?"

"I..." She faltered; words too hesitant to come out easily. "I saw your silhouette, okay? I didn't know what you were at first because the heavy canopies made it difficult to see. I knew that you weren't a bird, but I just didn't know what your intentions were. I thought you were stalking me or something."

"She's not wrong," Pistol quipped. "But she doesn't need to know about that."

"So, the first thing you decided to do was shoot me?" Reva exhaled deeply from her nostrils, observing the state of the woman. "You said it yourself. You didn't want to hurt anyone."

143

"I panicked, okay? My fight-or-flight reflex kicked in and I shot that arrow at you. I'm sorry." The woman glanced at her, probably observing her for wounds. "I'm glad you're alright."

"Thank you, I appreciate that." Reva winced, staring at her palms. A few scratches reddened, most likely due to how hastily she scaled down the tree after the scare. "What's your name?"

"Please," the woman replied, shaking her head. "Please don't report me to the police. I won't be able to take it."

"Huh?" Reva scrunched up her face in confusion. "I'm not reporting you to the police, silly. I just want to know your name."

"Really?" Cyrus leaned forward to catch Reva's gaze, but she tried not to look at him considering the mortal in front of her. "She almost killed you."

"And what if she killed that other dude?" Pistol suggested. "She has a trigger finger, she said it herself."

"Sybil Zimmerman," the woman admitted softly, and resumed pulling at her ankles. "I'm sorry that I did that to you. I really didn't mean it."

"If you were so willing to shoot me with an arrow, potentially killing me if it hit me, then how can I be so sure that you didn't already kill someone? Like Burton Crabb?"

Sybil's eyes widened with her words. Reva shrugged. "I mean, it's a genuine concern. Based on how you're looking at me right now, I can tell that you know who I'm talking about."

Blinking hard, Sybil let out a small noise. Her hands balled up, crumpling up the dry leaves underneath her. "I... I don't have anything to do with that man's murder. I promise you."

"You're the only person who I've encountered who knows how to work a bow and arrow pretty well. I'm not saying you did anything, but things don't look too good for you."

"No," Sybil said, shaking her head. "That's not true. There's plenty of people in Shadow Woods who can use a bow and arrow just as well as I can! Any one of them could have been responsible for Burton's death!"

Reva took a wild guess.

"Most of them don't have much of a history with him like you do, though." Crossing her arms over her chest, Reva nodded at the wide-eyed woman. "Am I right? Work with me, Sybil. Did you have anything to do with it?"

"No!"

"Do you know anyone who *might* have had something to do with it?"

"N-No! I swear!" Sybil's eyes started brimming with tears. "And what do you mean by history? I didn't like the man. I didn't want him near me."

At that, Reva frowned. "Why do you mean? I thought you were an ex-girlfriend of his."

"What?!" Sybil exclaimed, mouth ajar. "Who told you that? I despised Burton! I wanted nothing to do with him, but he kept trying to get something going! I avoided him as much as I could, but he somehow always managed to find me. Whoever told you that I had a relationship with him is wrong. Misguided, at least."

Huh. Reva considered that for a moment. Did that mean that Brenda lied to divert the investigation?

"So… you didn't have anything with Burton. No romance?" Reva pressed, hoping to clarify the situation.

To the side, Cyrus and Pistol watched on. The ghost leaned close to the familiar, keeping his voice level at a minimum.

"She's good at what she does, don't you think?"

Pistol stared at him. "Is this another one of your attempts at flirting with her? You're a little too obvious."

"I'm just trying to compliment her abilities in searching for the truth. She's determined to go after what she wants and doesn't stop until she gets it. That's admirable."

146

"Yeah, yeah. If you like her so much, why don't you just date her?"

"Huh?!" Cyrus recoiled, straightening out his clothing. "I… I don't think that would work, but…"

"Sure, it would," Pistol offered. "You're acting as if ghosts and humans haven't tried to have romantic relationships in the past."

"Seriously?"

"Why would I lie about this?" The familiar scoffed. "If anything, I shouldn't even be telling you about it. If you manage to start something more with her, you'll probably be more unbearable than you already are with your cheesy romance lines."

Meanwhile, Reva focused on the woman caught in the roots. Sybil struggled, and since she felt bad about pinning the roots so tightly around her ankles, Reva started helping her break free.

"I'll be honest with you, Sybil. I don't know if I can trust you."

"I feel the same way towards you," she replied. "That's probably because of how we're meeting each other, honestly."

"Yeah. You nearly killed me."

Heaving the roots off of Sybil, Reva managed to provide enough wiggle room that the other woman could slip her feet out of their hold. Once freed, Sybil sighed and flexed her legs. She stayed seated on the ground, Reva still standing over her.

"If you didn't kill Burton that night, where were you? What were you doing?"

"My alibi?" Sybil asked with a brief smile. "I was in town after finishing up work for the day. I don't know if I'm the person you should be focusing on... What was your name again?"

"Reva Brennan. Sorry." Offering her a hand, she lifted Sybil up to her feet. "Can you expand on what you just said? I still don't know if your alibi even exists."

"It does, I promise." Leaning over, Sybil gathered her bow, which had flown out of her hands when the roots snatched her legs. She organized the arrows that had fallen from her bag. "I own a shop where I keep all of my bows. A few days ago, probably a week ago, at this point, I noticed that one of the most powerful bows I owned went missing. I don't know what happened to it and I still haven't been able to find it."

"Did someone rob you?"

"Maybe," Sybil said, tossing her bag over her shoulder. "I barely used that thing. I mostly kept it up as a display, but it's gone."

The person who stole Sybil's bow… Maybe they had something to do with Burton's death?

"Do you have any idea who could have stolen it from you?"

"Not in the slightest. I never thought you'd have to worry about crimes like these in Shadow Woods, but hey." Sybil shrugged. "I guess we have to live with it now."

"Can I ask you for one more favor, Sybil?"

"I guess so."

"Can you take me to your shop?" Reva wrung her hands together. "Please?"

Chapter 22

After a bit of persuasion on Reva's part, Sybil agreed to lead her back towards Shadow Woods town square where the shop resided. They drove back in Reva's Jeep, with Sybil riding in the passenger seat while Pistol and Cyrus tagged along in the back. The duo stayed relatively quiet, not wanting to disturb Reva in her quest for the truth. However, Pistol hissed at Sybil when she tried to pet him.

"Is your shop close by?"

"A little ways off the center of town," Sybil answered.

Once exiting the more secluded parts of Shadow Woods, populated areas emerged on the horizon. With the former covered in heavy forestry and dirt paths, the latter featured paved roads, streetlights, and taller buildings.

Shadow Woods town square, just off the ocean, served as the *de facto* business center and the hot spot for individuals who wanted to find some excitement. Small restaurants and integral businesses scattered across the area. At the very center of the square, a large bronze monument of a lumberjack stood firm. Nicely trimmed shrubs, fountains, and parks added a sweet, hometown feel.

"Over there." Sybil pointed out a small building entitled *Timmy's Furs*. "I've partnered up with the guy. I hunt animals and bring him the pelts; he pays me for them."

Parking the car in a shaded spot, Reva followed Sybil into the establishment. Cyrus and Pistol stayed outside, chatting amongst themselves as they overlooked the busy streets of Shadow Woods.

A small bell chimed once they passed over the threshold of the shop, alerting the man with the newspaper behind the counter of their presence.

"Morning, Timmy," Sybil greeted, gripping tightly on the strap around her shoulder. She gestured to Reva. "This is Reva Brennan. We met a few minutes ago."

"In quite an adventurous way," Reva quipped, sending the woman a smile before turning towards Timmy. "I wanted to clarify some things with you, sir. I hope that's alright."

"Go on ahead, I'm listening." The man set aside his newspapers and crossed his arms over his chest, awaiting her questions.

"Was Sybil working with you the night prior to the police finding Burton Crabb's body in *The Yews* cemetery?"

"Whoa." Timmy glanced at Sybil. "What kind of mess did you get yourself into, young one?"

"Just tell her the truth, Timmy, I don't want to get caught up in this mess."

"Sybil stops by every night to drop off her hunt. She often works the whole day, finishes things off here, and returns home." Timmy recounted things with ease. "I could even show you the security footage of that night. See over there?"

Turning around and following his finger, Reva spotted a camera that pointed directly at the counter.

"That would show you what happened that night, as well as all the nights before. Say…" Timmy observed Reva curiously. "Are you a detective or something?"

"Nope. I'm just trying to clear my aunt's name. She's one of the suspects in the case and I'm trying to find the true killer before everything spirals out of control. That's why I wanted to make sure Sybil had nothing to do with it."

"Thank you for helping us out, Timmy," Sybil remarked, nodding his way. "Means a lot to me. I think I'll take the day off."

"You sure?"

"She's been through a lot," Reva explained, nudging at the woman's arm. "C'mon. Let's talk some more outside."

"You two take care now," Timmy called out, waving from the counter.

Once outside, Sybil and Reva leaned upon the building and stared into the street. Shoulder-to-shoulder.

"Do you believe me now?" Sybil asked, glancing her way.

"Sure, but I really hope you don't go off and shoot anymore people in the woods. Accident or not."

"That was a one-time thing."

"Yeah, and it could have landed you in jail if you hit me." Reva sighed, knocking the back of her head against the building. "Do you have a car?"

"No. I don't see the need for one. I get everywhere on foot."

Reva considered. She didn't think it was possible for Sybil to stop by *Timmy's Furs* that night, walk to *The Yews* five miles away, kill Burton, then escape on foot.

"Interesting," she whispered. "You know, when I heard about you, I really thought you were the one responsible for everything. It's probably because of the bow and arrow."

"I can't blame you for that." Sybil stuck her hands in her pockets. "Who told you about me?"

"Burton's ex-girlfriend. Brenda Braceling."

"Hmm. I've never heard of her."

"It's strange, I know." Reva sighed. "I'm starting to think she may be involved in his death, but I don't know for sure. She's leading me down false trails."

Somewhere to her left, she heard Cyrus and Pistol talking quietly about poems and novels. It surprised her, considering the familiar wasn't a particular fan of either one of those things.

Sybil spoke again. "Well, I can't say anything because I don't know the woman, but you should investigate her motives and whereabouts that night. I already proved where I was and what I was doing."

"Thank you for cooperating. You didn't have to," Reva pointed out. "I'm not even a detective or anything. I just... want to make sure the police leave my aunt alone."

"I understand. I don't have anything to worry about now that I've cleared my name, right?"

"Yep. And if some detective with shades pops up and starts asking you questions, let me know about it. I'll handle him."

"You've got a lot of influence, then?"

"I guess so."

Sybil stayed quiet, picking at a splinter in her index finger. Thinking back to their encounter in the forest, she looked at Reva again.

"How did those roots manage to trip me up so badly?" Sybil wondered aloud. "I didn't see them when I first approached that tree, but when I turned around, they were suddenly there."

"Maybe you just didn't notice them at first," Reva said, lying through her teeth. "It's not like they moved out of the ground themselves."

"Yeah... You have a point."

Somewhere to her side, she could hear Cyrus snickering at her comment.

Just as they were getting ready to head back to the car, they noticed a dark limousine round the town fountain and stopping before the town's historic theater. It had black-tinted windows, which hampered their ability to see the individual inside until they opened the door and popped their head out.

Donna Corona. Of course.

She entered the building with her chin held high, along with a new pair of sunglasses and a bodyguard at her side. Reva laughed quietly to herself.

"Do you know what she's up to?" she asked, motioning towards Donna's limo.

Sybil shook her head, pressing her lips tightly together.

"No, but it isn't the first time I've seen her driving around in that limo. She thinks she's better than all of us because her family has old money."

Reva nodded. That sounded right.

"I heard some rumors that she's trying to buy some town buildings," Sybil continued, leaning close to Reva. "I don't know how true it is, but it looks pretty likely. She might buy that building over there."

"The theater. Why would she do that?"

"She wants to own the town, I guess. I'm sure she wants to start off with the old, easier properties before moving onto the ones that are most coveted and expensive."

Like The Dimidio Inn, Reva thought to herself. *She won't get it.*

"That's not surprising," she admitted aloud.

"You know her?"

"Unfortunately."

"Sorry about that. She sounds like a pain to deal with." Sybil pushed off the building, readjusting her grip on the bag. "I'm glad we talked things through. I hope you find the person who killed Burton, because if it wasn't me and if it wasn't your aunt, then the murderer is somewhere out there still."

"I know. That's why I'm trying to act as quickly as possible."

"I didn't like him very much, but..." Shaking her head, Sybil offered a small smile. "You never want to see people turn up dead. I heard some details already. An arrow through the heart."

"Do you know about anyone who hated Burton enough to want to kill him?" Reva asked again, a shot in the dark at that point. "Anything can help, Sybil."

"I'm sorry," she replied. "I wasn't close to him. He was... *infatuated* with me somehow, but I didn't pay much attention to him. I wish I could help you there."

"Don't worry." Reva clapped a hand over her shoulder. "I appreciate everything you've done so far regardless of that."

Chapter 23

The next morning, after tending to their guests' needs, Reva and Cyrus decided to spend their time in *The*

Yews, playing a game of chess upon a blanket. They sat on a grassy section in the graveyard, comforted by the warm morning sun and the gentle breeze. Pistol showed up, too, pestering a ghost named Jackie.

Pistol saw ghosts with ease not because of his magical nature as a witch's familiar but because of his feline nature. All cats, from scrappy alley dwellers to pampered Persians, see and hear supernatural beings as easily as they see and hear one another.

Pistol considered that a perk. More beings gave him more targets for wit and mischief.

The cat's current target, Jackson Ayers Reynolds, died at twenty-two years old in a factory accident. Like most of the other spirits that occupied *The Yews*, Jackie found his time at the cemetery more enjoyable than the time in his mortal body.

"I just don't get it." With a flick of her finger, Reva used her magic to move her chess pieces across the board. One of her pawns captured Cyrus' rook. "I'm tired. This whole investigation has drained the life out of me."

"Then I invite you to join us at *The Yews*," Jackie offered, signaling across the graveyard with a hand.

"Not yet, Jackie. I don't have plans to do that for a very long time."

"Jackie, come look at this." Pistol held out his two front paws for the spirit. "Do you think the claws on this paw are longer than the ones on this one?"

"I think so. Why are you asking me that, kitty?"

"Because when I kill my next bird, I need to know which paw to lead with. Thanks!"

"Please don't bring your catches into the hotel," Cyrus said, sending him a pointed look. "After the snake incident, I feel as if we should just ban all animals from entering the inn for a while."

"Even *me*?!" Pistol exclaimed.

"Most definitely you."

"He's joking, Pistol," Reva reassured, knocking over Cyrus' queen piece with her knight. "But I may change my mind if you bring dirt into our establishment."

"Dramatic," the kitten mumbled, rolling his eyes.

"Reva, I'm sorry to point this out, but…" Jackie pointed at the area underneath her eyes. "It's getting dark under there. Have you been sleeping well?"

"Not really. During these last few nights, the investigation has been the only thing on my mind. I can't rest without thinking about the stupid thing or about how annoying that detective is."

Cyrus looked up, aimlessly moving his chess pieces around the board. He was never too good at the game, anyway. He liked watching, but he never understood the strategic importance of the moves.

"Have you heard from Alva?" Cyrus asked.

"Yeah, I haven't seen her around the cemetery in a while," Jackie added. "What happened to her? We all miss her. She gives us gifts and tells us stories."

"That detective called her in for another interrogation. I haven't heard much from her since and it's worrying me out of my mind. I don't know what to do."

"Relax!" Pistol bounded up to her. "She's probably at her cottage, knitting sweaters as we speak. I don't think that detective is dumb enough to do something to Alva. All eyes are on him right now."

"That's what I'm trying to convince myself of, too, but it's difficult sometimes." Running a hand through her hair, she stared miserably at her limp hair strands. "When this is all said and done, I think I'm going to have a full head of gray hair."

"Hey, if Alva can pull it off, you can, too," Jackie encouraged, sending her a smile. One of his front teeth was missing. "I agree with the kitty over there. I'm sure she's fine. Alva knows how to handle herself."

"And if we find out that the detective did anything to hurt her, we can retaliate!" Pistol suggested. Standing up on his hind legs, Pistol unsheathed his claws. "We can vandalize his house!"

"No," she deadpanned. "We absolutely cannot do that."

"Why not? It sounds like a fun idea, especially if you involve us spirits," Jackie said. "They won't be able to find much evidence of the perpetrator, don't you think? We don't have fingerprints, after all."

"He'll suspect that I had something to do with it. I'm probably the main person he's had an issue with since getting to Shadow Woods," Reva reasoned, finally knocking over Cyrus' king. "Checkmate."

"You're too good at this game," Cyrus said. "I didn't know I could move the queen more than one space across, but that's besides the point now. Pistol mentioned vandalizing that man's house and I got distracted."

"It's not a good idea."

"Says who?" Pistol challenged.

"The lawmakers who say that vandalism is a crime," she replied. "You're messing with a detective, remember? Someone who's part of the police force. I don't think we should go down that road, it's too dangerous."

"So how are you going to get your aunt out of this mess?" Jackie pressed, leaning forward. "Are you going to go teach that detective a lesson or what?"

"I'm trying to figure out the other suspects involved. So far, we've got three to work with other than Auntie Alva." Reva held up three fingers. "Sybil Zimmerman was the archer who nearly killed me yesterday, but I don't think she's the one responsible for Burton's death. Her story lines up well and I got the sense that she really didn't want anything to do with Burton."

"How do you know?" Cyrus questioned. "What if she's a good liar?"

"Her business partner, Timmy, corroborated her story. Plus, she told me that she doesn't have a car. It doesn't seem likely that she killed someone and then fled on foot. Someone would have seen her and this case would have been closed days ago."

"What about the other two?" Pistol nodded towards the fingers that she still kept upright. "That weird archer girl isn't the killer, so who is?"

"There's Mackie Crabb, his brother. I don't know much about him, but apparently, he fought with Burton on the day of his murder outside of his company offices. If he had some animosity towards Burton, that could have been enough to kill him. However, I don't know the nature of their relationship, so I can't tell."

Lastly, she left up a third finger. "Brenda Braceling."

"The woman from *Terror Tales*?" Cyrus brushed his mustache. "Why do you think she's involved?"

"I wonder if she's diverting attention off of herself by pointing fingers at Sybil and Mackie. She definitely had her reasons to see Burton dead. He was a lousy boyfriend to her, an even lousier boss, and with his death, she managed to obtain a higher position in their company."

"Ooh." Pistol sat on Jackie's lap, paying full attention. "She's suspicious. I can taste it."

"Ew," Jackie muttered.

"Reva, I'm glad that you're speaking candidly about the investigation, but I would like to mention some details about the hotel that you should consider," Cyrus said.

"Oh, no," she breathed out. "Did something else happen? Another snake?"

"No, not at all." Cyrus readjusted the collar of his jacket. "Earlier this morning, I overheard the two mortal guests in Room 4 complaining loudly about migraines. Now, I would like to believe that what they're experiencing is unrelated to the mysterious events surrounding the hotel, but I just wanted to let you know."

"You're dramatic," Pistol quipped. "Those people are probably just dehydrated."

"Or hungry," Jackie suggested. "I used to get like that when I didn't eat for too long."

"I'll check up on those guests and see if everything's alright with them," Reva reassured, patting Cyrus on the knee. "I can't afford bad reviews for the hotel right now. Burton's murder already made people feel uneasy about the area."

"I'm sure you'll figure things out. You always do," Cyrus pointed out, reorganizing the chess pieces on the board once more. "Would you like to play another round? I might lose, but I figure it's good practice."

Nodding, Reva watched as Cyrus set up the board. A pensive glaze spread over her eyes as she thought about the hotel. Something didn't feel right, and she wanted to tear her hair out at the thought that something evil lingered near them without her realizing it. If something horrible happened to anyone, Reva would blame herself.

She wanted her aunt's counsel, but felt wary about bringing her around the hotel while this presence remained in their midst. No matter how badly she wanted to figure out the truth, she drew the line at involving her aunt in situations that placed her health and wellbeing in peril. There had been too much of that already.

"Reva?" Cyrus waved a hand over her face. "Are you alright?"

Snapping out of her daze, she noticed Cyrus, Pistol, and Jackie staring at her curiously. She managed a smile, one that disappeared as quickly as it came.

"I'm great."

Chapter 24

The *Terror Tales* office building. Reva stared at it from her car, tapping her fingers against the steering wheel while she hummed a tune. From afar, she saw the sign on the front door read 'Closed' due to the employees' scheduled lunch break.

Leaning forward in her seat, Reva watched as a familiar face returned with a white shopping bag in her right hand. Brenda entered the building, flipped over the sign, and continued inside towards her office. In that moment, Reva unbuckled her seatbelt and raced after her, slipping inside before Brenda even had the chance to sit down at her desk.

"Hey!" Reva called out, which caused Brenda to stop in her tracks. "I need to talk to you."

"Is it about the investigation again?" Brenda slightly turned her body towards her, looking at her up and down, before continuing towards her office. "I already said everything I knew. I don't know what else you need to hear from me."

"I spoke with Burton's ex-flame you mentioned."

Halting her movements, the woman reacted slowly to Reva's claim. She set her bag down on her desk, then gripped at the back of her chair tightly.

"Did you?"

"Her name is Sybil Zimmerman. She's an archer and she hunts in the Shadow Woods forest as a part of her job."

"...I'm glad you found her." Sliding her chair, Brenda plopped down and reached into one of her drawers. She pulled out another one of those phone wire bracelets. "Here, would you like one? I have too many of these lying around."

"These again?" Reva took it from her hand. "Did the same woman sell them to you?"

"Natalie Owens, yes. She's so happy that *Terror Tales* is finally correcting all the lies Burton perpetuated about her family that she sent me another batch of bracelets, for free this time. I'm giving them out to nearly everyone I see."

"Thanks." Pocketing the bracelet, Reva made the move to sit across Brenda's desk. "You were mistaken about Sybil being Burton's ex-flame. According to her, they weren't even close. He was infatuated with her, but the feelings weren't mutual."

"Miss Brennan, I'm afraid to say that I don't want to talk about this investigation anymore." She took her time folding her hands over her desk. "I'm tired of talking about Burton. May he rest in peace and all that, but I'd like to forget about his memory sooner rather than later."

"I understand how you feel, Brenda, but you need to see things from my perspective. I'm trying to find the killer."

165

"You don't have to, you know. The lead detective of the Shadow Woods Police Department is already taking charge of this case. I don't know why you're so adamant on finding the answers for yourself."

"I don't trust that he's doing the right thing," she admitted, planting her palm on Brenda's desk. "I'm doing my own research to find out who killed Burton, and I'm not going to stop until I figure this one out."

Sighing, Brenda leaned her head against her hand. She stared at Reva, looking tired.

"Alright. What do you need to know?"

"Where were you the night that Burton was killed?"

Eyes narrowing, Brenda scowled. "Seriously?"

"I want to make sure that you're not a suspect. It's nothing personal. I asked Sybil the same question and she introduced me to a friend who corroborated her story. That's why I'm sure that she didn't have anything to do with it."

Exasperated, Brenda motioned towards her office door. "I worked overtime the night it happened. I didn't leave this building until around two o'clock in the morning. There's no chance I could have driven to *The Yews*, killed Burton, come back, and slept enough to be coherent the next day. Just not possible."

Reva nodded. "And your alibi–"

"You can ask Lola when she gets back from her lunch break. Is that all you wanted to know?"

She stayed silent, drumming her foot against the floor as she tried to think of something else to ask. Her trip appeared less than fruitful. Brenda didn't put up much of a fight answering her questions, although she could tell that the woman seemed agitated. She didn't like the investigation, but neither did Reva.

"Did you hate Burton?"

"Why would you ask me that?"

"Out of curiosity. Based on the way you speak about him; it seems like you do."

"Well, I won't head to the police station and announce that I'm happy he's dead because they'll figure I had something to do with things." Brenda scratched at her forearm, shaking her head. "I won't miss him, though."

"Your relationship turned out *that* badly with him?"

"Over these last few days, I've thought about what we used to have. I'm glad it's all over because I didn't deserve to get treated like that." Tucking a strand behind her hair, she sighed. "No one does."

"I'm sorry," Reva whispered. "I didn't mean to pry."

"I remember feeling so scared to stand up to him for anything. My stomach would hurt, my hands would shake, I

167

would nearly be on the verge of crying before anything came out of my mouth. Ridiculous."

"Did this happen when you mentioned his lies on the ghost tours?"

"It happened before any argument, really. He always made me feel as if I was crazy for bringing up these concerns with him. By the end of the relationship, I stopped mentioning things that bothered me altogether. I felt it wasn't worth it if I was going to get ignored or belittled for it."

"Sybil didn't like him either, by the way." Reva trailed her finger along the armrest, waiting for Brenda's reaction. "She didn't want anything to do with him."

A dry laugh followed. "Smart girl," Brenda remarked. "I feel free now that he isn't my boss anymore. He turned into more of an ogre once the relationship ended."

"What about his brother?" Reva pressed. "You mentioned him back at the police station while you talked with Detective Carver. What do you know about him?"

"He's a deadbeat, through and through. He fought often with Burton because of their family inheritance or whatever. Apparently, their parent's home was supposed to be shared between them, but since Mackie didn't have a job and couldn't contribute, Burton threw him out of the house."

"His own brother? He just left him to fend for himself!"

"Considering this is Burton we're talking about; I wasn't too surprised to hear about it. Mackie's been angry ever since. Like I said to the detective, I saw them fighting outside of this building. Hours later, Burton's found dead in the cemetery. Mackie may have had something to do with things."

"Do you know where I can find him?"

"No, I'm sorry." Brenda frowned. "Last time I heard, he wanders through Shadow Woods because he doesn't have a home or the money to rent a room anywhere. He's pretty lost in the world at the moment, so I couldn't tell you where he was even if I tried."

"And you told Detective Carver about him?"

Brenda nodded. "So I assume that he already knows about Mackie and is probably out there looking for him?"

"If he's as good a detective as people make him out to be, I'd hope so. I'm pretty sure Mackie is purposely lying low and avoiding the police. They often catch him for public intoxication or for being a nuisance in general."

"That's a sad life to live." Reva pushed herself out of the seat, dusting out her pants. "Thank you for speaking to me about this, Brenda. I appreciate it. Do you have any future tours planned for *The Yews* any time soon?"

"I'm pretty sure we do!" Brenda turned to her desktop, pulling up a calendar as well as a schedule. "Within the next three weeks, actually. Why do you ask?"

Shrugging, Reva walked over to the doorway and leaned on it.

"It'll be interesting to see how well your tours perform now that Burton isn't around to embellish stories about the dead. I hope everything turns out alright."

"Actually, our business has been booming ever since he was found murdered. It's strange. In the past, when rumors about his shady behavior spread through town, it ruined our reputation and clients stayed away. Now his demise has actually boosted sales." Brenda paused, rationalizing things in her mind. "There's a silver lining to everything, I suppose."

"You're really turning things around with this company. It's refreshing to see."

"Yeah, well…" She leaned back in her seat. "You can accomplish a lot once toxic people are cut out of your life, in one way or another."

Chapter 25

Reva made her way back towards the inn from the *Terror Tales* office and wondered how she was going to find Burton's brother Mackie. If he was even half as mysterious as Brenda insinuated he was, then he'd be harder to find than a

170

needle in a haystack. Still, she had to try. She needed more leads, and if finding Mackie was how she'd accomplish that, then she'd better get cracking.

She was so lost in thought that she almost didn't see Detective Carver sitting by the small fountain in the center of the cemetery, holding a takeout cup of coffee. Once she did, though, she sighed and looked around. He didn't seem to notice her so she could avoid talking to him if she wanted, which was a tempting thought. There was something about him though, about the way he was just sitting there all alone, that made her want to stop. It was almost like something was pulling her towards him. Intuition, maybe? So, she decided to trust her gut, and called out to him as she got closer.

"Detective Carver!"

He looked up and over at her, clearly a bit startled. "Hello."

As she made her way towards him, she cocked her brow, and placed one hand on her hip as she spoke. "What are you doing here?"

"I've got as much right as anyone else in this town to visit public property, don't I?"

She rolled her eyes at the way he bristled back at her and wondered why he had to be so curmudgeonly about everything. Didn't he realize that the nicer he was, the more willing people would be to cooperate with him? Just because

171

he was easy on the eyes didn't mean that he could act like a jerk and expect people not to react accordingly. Just as she opened her mouth to say as much he spoke, but this time his voice was softer, almost gentle.

"I don't know, I just…" He went quiet for a few seconds and she watched as he shrugged his shoulders, like he was trying to figure out how to say what he wanted to say. "Since I got here, I've been trying to do some research on the town and its people. Including your family."

Okay so she hadn't expected that. She nodded and listened on with curiosity, leaning against a stone fence pillar as she did.

"Honestly, your family history is impressive. Everything that you've overcome and accomplished… it's inspiring, really."

As much as Reva liked to hear that maybe Detective Jerkface didn't have it out for her quite as much as he had previously, she was still wary of him reading her family's history. Not that she or her family were bad people of course, but they were… different. There were certain things that Matt Carver just didn't need to know about the Brennans.

Specifically, they had certain *talents* that regular people didn't. The family's magical nature was something that they didn't go flaunting around, especially not to detectives who could potentially ruin their lives. Reva didn't trust him enough to order her coffee, let alone keep a secret like that.

So, she promptly changed the subject. "What happened with my Aunt Alva?"

That seemed to bring Carver back to reality and he nodded, gesturing vaguely with his hands. "Oh, she's fine. I escorted her myself back to her cottage, so I would imagine that's where she still is."

That surprised her, if she was being honest. She'd expected him to do everything he could to keep her aunt there for questioning. "You brought her home? Just like that?"

He shrugged his shoulders with a sigh, nodded his head, and sipped his coffee. "Well, yeah, just like that. We couldn't really prove anything. Plus, it's not like she hasn't been cooperative with us." He leaned back on the bench he was sitting on, gazing out across the cemetery as he spoke. "She admitted to the fact that her fingerprints were on his jacket, and she was upfront about how they got there. She and Burton had a couple of run-ins in the graveyard, and she'd tried to physically push him off the property more than once. That lines up with what we've been told and with the evidence we have so far. So, I brought her back to her cottage."

It was a bit of a shock that the Detective had simply let her aunt go without trying to press her harder or finding a reason to keep her detained. Reva figured that he would have done everything in his power to find an excuse to keep her there or pin the murder on her. What was really bothering her, though, was the fact that her aunt had gotten herself so tangled up in this mess in the first place. Why would she admit to *anything*? It was almost like she was asking for trouble. Surely her aunt had done nothing wrong, but that didn't mean that she didn't need to be cautious.

"Oh. I see."

He turned to look at her then, frowning. "You seem surprised."

"I'll be honest, I am." She tilted her head and fiddled with her nails, brow furrowed. "I just assumed that you'd be dogging her for a while since you seemed so bent on involving her in some way. Getting a win on your books, and all that jazz."

He scoffed and shook his head. "I'm bent on finding the truth and the real killer. Just because I'm thorough and investigate every possible avenue doesn't mean that I'm a crooked cop, you know."

Okay, so maybe she had been a bit hard on him. She still didn't trust him, but at least he seemed to care about actual justice and not just making himself look good.

"Fair enough."

"Besides, we still haven't been able to find the bow used as the murder weapon. And," he said as he finished his

174

coffee with a sigh. "There's still the matter of the second set of prints on Burton's jacket."

He grumbled and tucked his hands into his pockets, and Reva actually found herself wondering if maybe Detective Carter wasn't so bad after all. She stood a bit closer and relaxed her stance, an amused smirk playing on her features.

"Why are you telling me all this? Earlier you couldn't seem to get rid of me fast enough."

He shrugged his shoulders looking almost defeated, gazed back at her.

"I guess because I don't really have anyone else to talk to about it."

That surprised Reva. She knew what it was like to feel that way, as did most people who had secrets they'd sworn to keep. She thought for a moment. Would it really be so bad to be nice to Detective Jerkface and help him solve this, rather than trying to outdo him behind his back? At the very least it would help get her aunt off the hook, right?

She decided right then and there that despite the fact that she had an uneasy feeling about it, she was going to help him solve the case.

Though she should probably refrain from calling him Detective Jerkface from here on out.

"Well, Detective Carver," Reva said with a smile, "Now you do have someone to talk to."

Chapter 26

Since Reva figured that helping Detective Carver, or *Matt* as he asked her to call him, was in her best interest, she got right down to business and told him everything she knew. If she was going to clear her aunt's name as a suspect as well as find out who the real murderer was, then she couldn't leave anything out.

Having said that, Matt wasn't exactly pleased to hear that she had been spying on people while hiding in the trees. She sat down next to him on the concrete cemetery bench and started to tell him what she'd learned.

"You could have gotten shot, you know, if the real murderer came across you."

Hoo boy, if he only knew.

"Funny you should mention that…"

He blanched and turned his body towards her. His eyes narrowed and his brow furrowed in a way that made her almost smile, but she managed to hold back. "Please don't say that you actually got shot and you're only *now* just telling me."

Reva chuckled softly and shook her head. The relief that washed over him as he whooshed out a sigh made her giggle turn into a laugh, though, and she shook her head. He wasn't nearly as amused.

"This isn't funny, Reva!"

"It's a *little* funny. Besides, I'm fine, I didn't actually get shot. I got shot *at*, but the person missed. And it all worked out in the end because I got some info I wouldn't have had otherwise!"

He dragged his hand down over his face with a nod and gestured for her to keep talking.

"Anyway I was sitting up in the tree with Pistol-"
"Pistol?"

"Yes, Pistol. My cat. Can I continue? Or are you going to keep interrupting me before I can actually get anything out?"

He huffed and waved her on, leaning back against the bench as he listened.

"As I was saying… I was sitting in the tree with Pistol and I heard a noise. I turned to look and just barely dodged out of the way in time. Someone had fired an arrow right at me in the tree!"

This clearly caught his attention and he suddenly sat forward; eyes focused on her. She felt a bit smug that she could make a detective hang on the edge of her words like that, but that was neither here nor there. She kept going.

"Anyway, I managed to catch myself, but I almost fell out of the tree. As I was holding onto the branch and pulling myself up, the shooter stumbled and tripped on some tree roots and branches. They fell right into the dirt, face first."

"Well, that was lucky."

She nodded. He didn't need to know the fact that Cyrus had helped her stay in the tree and that she'd used her powers to trip her assailant. There was enough rough and uneven ground in Shadow Woods for anyone to trip, let alone someone running away after having been caught. He didn't seem to be suspicious of anything she'd said so far, so she kept going.

"Anyway, I ran over to the person with the bow and arrow and pinned them down and made them face me."

"I'm going to ignore the fact that you could probably be charged with assault for that but keep going."

"Ugh, just let me tell my story. Anyway. The woman who shot at me was Sybil Zimmerman, Burton's rumored ex-flame."

Once again, his interest was clearly captured and she smiled, nodding.

"Right? I thought for sure that she had to be the one who had done it. After all she did shoot at me with a bow and arrow, but she's not the one we're looking for. It turns out that she shot at me because she thought that someone was stalking her."

"Well, she was kind of right, wasn't she? You were waiting for her in the tree."

"That's beside the point."

He rolled his eyes again and sighed. "Alright, tell me why she's not a viable suspect?"

"Because she had an alibi. She was in that shop run by the old guy, the one who sells pelts, Timmy. Anyway, she said was there until almost 2AM, and he backed her up. But get this:" She leaned closer again, brows raised. "One of the more powerful bows from her shop was stolen a few nights before the attack. She figures that the thief took the bow to kill Burton. And!" she added excitedly, her voice hushed. "I found out that Burton and his brother had a huge fight right before he was killed. The very same day. I'll bet that the second set of fingerprints you're trying to identify are his."

Matt took a deep breath and shook his head, clearly trying to make sense of it all. It was barely a moment later when he looked back at Reva, his eyes narrowed and his voice low. "And how exactly did you come across all of this information?"

Uh oh, busted. Reva shrugged her shoulders and looked back at him, wondering what his endgame was. "It doesn't matter. Look, I'm not trying to meddle, I just want to clear my aunt's name. I know that she had nothing to do with this."

"Of course, it matters! This is police business, Reva!" He muttered under his breath and then looked back at her, his lips pursed with frustration. "You've got to cut this out. You're going to get yourself hurt or mess up the investigation."

"Uh, no, I'm absolutely not going to do that. This is my aunt's reputation we're talking about, not to mention the fact that there's a killer out there! No, I'll stop once we find out who *actually* killed Burton, and once the investigation is over."

With that she crossed her arms over her chest and stared back at Matt, who looked stunned.

He opened his mouth to argue with her and she glared, shaking her head. He seemed to realize that arguing was no use, though, because he relented quickly enough. Good. After a moment he threw his hands up with a huff and shrugged. "Fine. Whatever. I'll try and find Burton's brother to bring him in for questioning. But in the meantime,' he added as he squinted and pointed his finger at her. "You need to keep your nose out of this and stay out of my way. I need to make sure that this is done by the book so that if this is the guy we're looking for, I can get him. I don't want your interference to cost me this case. Understand?"

"Sure, fine."

He grumbled as he stood up and said his goodbyes. Reva watched him walk away and then left the bench herself and headed back towards the inn. She smiled when she saw Cyrus, though the smile faltered when he spoke.

"I heard you talking to him, you know. I don't see how working with him is going to help anything. Don't you remember how rude he was to you?"

"Of course I do, but things seem different. Plus, he seems to care about finding the actual killer, not just pinning it on anyone to look good. Maybe I was wrong about his motives."

Cyrus rolled his eyes with a scoff. "Oh, so are you two best friends now?"

Man, what was up with Cyrus? Reva shook her head with a frown and wondered what had got his feathers so ruffled.

"Of course not, but if helping Matt is going to clear my aunt's name and keep her out of jail, then so be it."

"Oh it's *Matt* now, is it? Well, don't let me intrude on your relationship with your new favorite person. Excuse me."

She waved him off with a frustrated huff and walked past him, wondering why he was in such a tiff. Shouldn't he be happy about the fact that Matt was no longer considering

181

her aunt the prime suspect? Either way, she wasn't going to let Cyrus' bad mood get to her.

Because despite the fact that she told Matt she wouldn't interfere, she absolutely was not going to sit back and leave the digging to everyone else. She had some investigating to do.

Chapter 27

Reva's night was less than restful, and she barely slept. She was plagued with nightmares and anxiety. If she wasn't worrying about her aunt's fate and whether or not she'd be going to jail, she was having a nightmare about the fact that her hotel seemed to be coming apart at the seams.

But would it even matter if it was? After all, it seemed like Donna was particularly focused on buying out all of the businesses and drowning out everyone else who wouldn't sell. How could she stay afloat and keep her hotel if that vile woman was so determined to break her?

On top of that, she was worried about whether or not Matt was really on her side. Was helping him a bad idea? What if Cyrus was right and she was making a huge mistake in working with Matt? Would everything come crashing down around her?

Regardless of how many times she vowed to relax and sleep, her mind always went back to delving into every worry she had.

She actually managed to doze off a bit after she heard the sounds of the birds chirping and singing their morning songs. It didn't last long though, because no sooner had she started to drift off than Pistol pounced onto her bed. She let out a surprised gasp when he trotted over to her, sharp teeth on display in a grin.

"And why are you so happy so early in the morning?"

"Because! I caught a mouse earlier, while you were still lazing about in bed."

She yawned and stretched her arms above her head, and tried to rub the sleep from her eyes as she murmured into her pillow.

"Uh huh, that's great Pistol. I'm still so tired. I barely slept."

She was just about to tell him to leave her be so she could try and catch some more shut eye, when the sound of a loud crash against her bedroom wall filled the room.

"What the-"

She nearly fell out of bed as she scrambled to catch herself. Her eyes went wide with shock and Pistol hissed and jumped back, darting around next to her with his fur and hackles raised.

"Uh, I'm not sure about you Reva, but that didn't sound good to me."

Well that was the understatement of the year. There was no *good* reason she could think of as to why there would have been something hitting her wall. The sound was loud enough to startle her completely awake and it was coming from outside. What on Earth could have hit the hotel?

She quickly grabbed the cardigan sweater that had been hanging off of her bedpost and threw it around her shoulders. Then she darted down the hall and outside to investigate what could have possibly hit the wall. It wasn't like things hitting the hotel were a regular occurrence, so she didn't even know what she was looking for. Had a sign fallen and hit the siding, maybe? It was possible, she supposed, though it had never happened since she had been running the hotel. Had another local kid thrown a rock against the building?

In any case, she needed to find out what it was. Something *that* loud wasn't ever good.

It only took her moments to get outside, Pistol in tow, trotting quickly behind her. It was early so the air still had that morning crispness, and she wrapped her sweater tightly around her with a shudder. Then she jogged around to where her bedroom window was.

She stopped dead, gasping in horror.

She wasn't sure what she was expecting to see but it certainly *wasn't* this. She couldn't help the way that her eyes went wide with shock as she stepped closer to the wall.

Pistol crept up behind her, scowling.

"Is that what I think it is?"

She nodded down at him and then crept forward; her brow furrowed. Pinned to the wall of the hotel was a dove, a knife stabbed straight through its heart. The blood was a bright crimson in contrast to the siding and the bird's white feathers.

Whose idea of a sick joke was this? Stabbing an innocent animal, for one, and then pinning it to the side of the hotel? Someone took a life to send a message, and an unclear one, at that.

She couldn't help but think that this was somehow related to the snake that she had found in the vent. Of course it was, that would be too large of a coincidence. The thought of it made her feel physically ill and her stomach was in knots.

Maybe she actually had a serious problem.

"Need a hand cleaning that up?"

She yelped and jumped backwards at the sound of Cyrus standing right behind her. She hadn't even heard or felt him approach, she had been so distracted. "Cyrus! You scared me nearly to death."

"Well," he chortled with a wink. "At least you're in the right place for it."

She glared back at him and he cleared his throat, and muttered an apology.

"Too soon for jokes, Cyrus. And yes," she added with a heavy sigh, "I would love some help. I have a dozen things I need to do today, and I'd rather not add to the list."

She turned to face her friend then, not trying to sound ungrateful for his help. She truly didn't know where she'd be without him.

"Thank you, I mean that."

Cyrus nodded and then turned on his heel, presumably to go and get supplies. Then Reva turned to take another glance at the poor bird impaled on her wall. Pistol spoke up then, his soft fur rubbing gently against her leg as he did.

"You know I've had an odd sort of feeling around the hotel for quite some time now. I had been brushing it off, but I don't think I should do that anymore."

She tilted her head with a frown and focused on Pistol, her curiosity piqued.

"A feeling? What kind?"

"The feeling that I should be careful. It's unsettling. I'd like to think that the bird has nothing to do with it, but... I don't think that's wise. There seems to be too much going on for it not to be related, right?"

She nodded and absentmindedly ran her fingers over the siding, stopping short of where the dove's blood had started to dry. There was only one person in the world that she could turn to about this, and one person only. The only one who she felt absolutely safe with, and who she knew that she could talk to about anything. There was no one else, really.

"Come on Pistol, let's go inside and get dressed. I need to talk to Aunt Alva."

Chapter 28

She caught herself accidentally speeding through Shadow Woods in her hasty attempt to reach her aunt's cottage. A gnawing feeling hounded her as she drove through the small streets and dirt trails that led the way towards her door. Her stomach twisted itself up, though she couldn't pinpoint the exact reason why.

Seeing her aunt's cottage and its familiar floral surroundings allowed her to breathe deeply at last. Reva parked her car in a spot not too far from the cottage's porch. Then, she quickly leapt up the front steps and knocked a few times, hoping that her jitters weren't warranted.

"Auntie?" More knocks came. "It's me, Reva! I wanted to talk to you about something important. Can I come in?"

She waited patiently for a response, but it never came. Reva tried looking through the windows to see if her aunt was just too busy in the kitchen to come to the door, but the curtains hampered her ability to see inside.

Instead of waiting outside, Reva checked underneath the potted plant on her aunt's porch, which was where she kept the spare key. She nearly fumbled and dropped the key as she unlocked the handle, pushing her way inside noisily to encounter an empty living room.

"Auntie?" Reva called out, setting the key down in a small porcelain glass holder near the door. "Auntie, where are you? I've…" She made her way in, peeking around to see any signs of life. "Where is she?"

Checking all the rooms, from the master bedroom to the guest bedroom as well as every room in between, Reva's breathing rate accelerated with the realization that her aunt wasn't in the cottage. The worst possible scenarios started trickling into her thoughts, causing her to pace around the living room as she considered what to do next.

She paused for a moment and sent a flurry of texts to Alva. She dialed her cell, but it went straight to voicemail. Dead ends.

Time for the big guns.

Reva gripped the back of the couch and focused on the magic seeping through her body. Closing her eyes tightly, she channeled that power into a distress call that traveled for miles to reach its intended targets. Her knees nearly buckled afterwards since the spell caused a sudden depletion of her energy.

She sat to wait, head in her hands, on the living room couch. After a short while, multiple knocks sounded, along with some light scratching along the front door's bottom edge.

Cyrus and Pistol stood upon the porch, eyes wide with concern and confusion.

"What happened, Reva? Are you alright?" Cyrus made his way in, observing her thoroughly to see if there were any signs of struggle. "Did someone hurt you?"

"N-No, not at all, but…" Reva did a double-take between the two. "How did you guys get here so fast? I didn't expect you so quickly!"

"You act as if we're not crafty," Pistol quipped, coming in to sit on the couch. "We saw a pickup truck outside *The Dimidio Inn* around the same time you sent us that distress signal. All we had to do is hop in the bed and stay quiet until the driver got us close enough to hop out. Then, we finished the walk all the way here. It didn't take too long, to be honest."

"We came as soon as you sent the signal," Cyrus added, placing a hand on her shoulder. "Why did you do it? What's happening?"

"I…" Reva sighed shakily, running a hand across her face. "I can't find my aunt. I already searched her entire cottage, but I can't find her. She's not answering my texts and my calls can't even go through."

"What if she's out buying groceries or something?" Pistol asked, stretching out his paws. "She could be at the library or talking to some friends."

"I don't think so," Reva replied. "I wouldn't be feeling this weird if I thought the same thing. I'm trying to calm myself down, but I really think something happened to her."

Seeing her become more upset, Cyrus wrapped an arm around her to comfort her. Then, he spoke.

"We'll continue looking around the cottage to find any clues about her whereabouts," he assured, rubbing circles in her shoulder with his thumb. "Pistol, can you help me look outside? Maybe we'll see something interesting."

"I really hope we're not just overreacting," the familiar said, already bounding out the door. "She could be window-shopping in town or something. She's an adventurous one, after all."

190

"I want to believe that, but…" Reva shook her head, rubbing at her eyes until she saw colors. "There's something else going on. I know there is."

Reva continued calling Aunt Alva's phone as Cyrus and Pistol combed the area around the cottage. Similarly to Reva, they didn't find anything that could point them in the right direction. When they came back inside with the news, Reva felt her hope dwindling down to ashes.

"Reva, I promise you that everything will be alright with your aunt," Cyrus began, closing the front door once Pistol made his way inside. "She can't be far. Shadow Woods isn't a big region."

"Something happened to her." Reva sniffled loudly into her fist, unable to stop the tears from forming. "I-I don't know where she is. She's not at home, she's not at the inn or *The Yews*, so I… I don't know."

"She has some friends in town who she visits, right?" Cyrus asked gently, taking hold of her shoulders. "What if she's out having some tea? Catching up with acquaintances? Those are all possibilities."

"I wouldn't feel so bad if she would just *reply* to my messages, Cyrus." Glancing at her phone screen, she hoped that the device would light up with the notification of a text or call. Nothing came. "She doesn't usually do this. She always replies whenever I text or call her."

"Maybe her device died," he offered. "You shouldn't worry so much, my beloved. It's not good for your health."

"Uh..." Pistol turned around from the fireplace he stared at. "Guys? Can you come here for a second? I found something weird in the fireplace."

Reva dashed over, nearly tripping over her own feet. Crouching beside Pistol, she peered into the small space and tried to identify what he referred to. "What, Pistol? What did you find?"

"That white thing," the familiar replied, nodding in its general direction. "It looks like a piece of paper, but it's folded up. It's not crumpled or burnt by the fire, so someone might have put it there recently."

"Let me see," Cyrus said, reaching beneath the blackened logs and pulling out a small, folded note. "He's right. The paper is still crisp, so it appears relatively unused."

"Give me the note," she demanded, and Cyrus quickly complied.

Unfolding the paper, she held it tightly in her hands. The handwriting. She recognized Aunt Alva's words. The note's contents ripped a strangled gasp from her throat.

I knew you would look for me, Reva, so I left this behind to tell you that I did it for your own good. I didn't want to see you hurt. I'm sorry.

"What does… What does she mean by this…?" Reva asked despondently, clutching the note in her hands. "What did she do?!"

"Reva, calm down," Cyrus pleaded. Pistol looked on with a frightened gaze, his typical jesting demeanor quelled by the gravity of the situation. "We should think about things critically before we jump to conclusions–"

"No." Reva rose from her seat beside the fireplace, wiping away at her eyes. "I'm going to the police station and I'm going to ask if they have any information about my aunt's whereabouts. If they don't, I'll file a missing person's report."

"I can come with you, if you'd like," Pistol offered, standing as tall as he could. "I don't want to think something bad happened to Alva, but…"

"Are you sure?" Cyrus asked, frowning. "Do you really want to do this?"

"I have no other choice, Cyrus! My aunt is missing, and she's done something serious!" Reva snapped, bunching up her hands. "I don't want to wait any longer. What if she's in danger and we're wasting time?"

"I see," he replied, somewhat taken aback by her tone and behavior towards him. "In that case, I can return to the inn and take care of the establishment. I hope you two stay safe while you do so."

Nodding, Reva scooped Pistol up in her arms.

"We'll see you later then, Cyrus."

Chapter 29

At the police station, the receptionist's eyes widened once she saw Reva and Pistol walking through the entrance. She straightened up in her seat, stopping her work to assist an obviously-agitated Reva. "Hello, ma'am."

"Miriam, is it?" Reva asked, leaning briefly on the counter. "I need to speak with Detective Matt Carver, please. It's an urgent matter."

"I'll check if he's available." Brief typing followed, as well as a few clicks as she navigated through schedules and appointments. "He doesn't have any meetings for this time slot, so I believe–"

That was all Reva needed to hear before she made her way down the same route as before towards his office. She left the receptionist talking to herself but considering the last time she tried to stop Reva from entering the detective's office didn't work out too well, Miriam stayed planted in her seat and continued working.

When Reva entered the office, she pressed Pistol tightly against her chest to prevent the familiar from hopping onto the detective's desk. Matt sat in front of his laptop, updating the details of a case with a manila folder opened beside him. He glanced up, but his lack of expression marked his indifference.

The softness she'd seen in him the day before had fallen away. Detective Jerkface was back. "I had a feeling you would show up sometime today," he remarked, leaning back in his chair. "Would you like to take a seat and talk calmly? Or do you prefer shouting, like you usually do?"

"What are you talking about?" Reva asked, narrowing her eyes. "I came to talk to you about my aunt, but–"

"I know."

Pistol growled. Reva felt the low vibrations against her chest as the familiar appeared ready to pounce out of her arms. Matt observed her pensively.

"I can understand you're upset," he said, after a long period of tense silence. "Believe me, I wasn't expecting this outcome, either."

"What are you even talking about?" Reva sat on one of the seats across from his desk, still holding tightly onto Pistol before he lashed out.

"He thinks we're stupid or something," the familiar grumbled out, watching the detective's movements with pointed interest. "I'm going to bite him."

Reva tapped on his body, hoping that he would calm down.

"You wanted to speak to me about your aunt, correct?"

195

"Yes, I..." Reva's mind raced to rationalize the situation. How did he know? What *happened*? "I wanted to talk to you because I can't find her. She hasn't responded to my calls or texts, and I visited her cottage already and I couldn't find her anywhere. I–"

"Well, of course she's not going to answer any of your calls," he interjected in a matter-of-fact tone. "People don't have access to their phones while they're in a jail cell, you know."

At that moment, Reva felt her heart drop. Her grip on Pistol loosened momentarily, but it gave the familiar enough time to vault himself upon Matt's desk and crash onto his keyboard.

"Idiot detective! How dare you talk to us like that? Who do you think you–"

Matt grabbed Pistol by the scruff, observing the loud kitten with a stern glare. Although the familiar went limp, he continued shouting insults at Matt, but the detective only heard meows.

"Does your cat always behave like this?"

"Let him go." Reva's grip tightened on the armrest. Her words sounded oddly calm. "Why is my aunt in a jail cell?"

Matt's eyes widened briefly. He, perhaps, expected to get into yet another yelling fit with the Brennan woman who had served as a thorn in his side ever since he stepped foot into Shadow Woods. She patiently waited for his response, even crossing her legs.

"I'm glad we can go about this calmly," he began, smiling. "Your aunt came to us earlier today and confessed to the murder of Burton Crabb.

"I don't understand why she did that, considering we have no evidence that directly incriminates her, but I accepted her confession."

"What?!" Reva shot up out of her chair.

"Here we go," Matt whispered to himself.

"What do you *mean* she confessed to his murder?! That makes no sense! She already told me that she didn't have anything to do with it!"

"Reva, please calm down. I already told you that I'm trying to make sense of everything that happened as well. Things don't line up correctly–"

"Then *why* is she in a jail cell?!"

"Reva." Matt stood from his seat, towering over her. Pistol continued yowling his insults from below, but the detective ignored him. "I need you to allow this process to proceed without interruptions. I don't need any issues from here on out, especially now that the investigation is coming to a close–"

"No, it isn't, because she isn't the killer!" Reva exclaimed. "Something happened to her. She didn't make that statement on her own accord, I *know* this."

"I'm going to figure out if that's true or not. For now, we have to–"

"And what about Mackie Crabb? Burton's brother? Brenda said that he punched Burton outside of *Terror Tales* on the day of his murder. How do we know that he didn't go back during the night and finish the job in *The Yews*?"

"Based on the evidence and eyewitness testimony I've received, that's impossible."

"Why?"

"For one, we've already booked Mackie Crabb, but for another reason. An officer found him publicly intoxicated near the town square, so he's getting charged for that. However, he's not going to be charged with Burton's murder because a witness saw him passed out drunk in front of a local bar on the night that Burton was killed."

With each word, Reva felt hope depleting rapidly from her body. She tried to keep a brave face for Alva's sake, but it was difficult. Mind-numbingly difficult.

"Because of these developments, your aunt is the only suspect left in the investigation without an alibi to corroborate her whereabouts on the night Burton was killed."

"She was in her cottage."

"How do you know that?"

"She's my *aunt*. Of course, I'm going to know where she is!"

"Well, you didn't know where she was just moments prior to this conversation," he pointed out.

He hadn't meant it to sound like a taunt, but Reva took it as one. Swallowing hard, she bit her tongue hard enough to draw blood.

"Reva, I don't think there's much we can do here," Pistol said, standing on the edge of the desk. "We can't just break her out!" The familiar paused. "I mean, we can, but there's too many witnesses and it would be difficult."

"This isn't fair," she said quietly. "None of it is. My aunt didn't kill him."

"There's not much else I can say. Her confession makes things difficult for her."

Aunt Alva, what did you do? Reva despaired, feeling a migraine settling in her temples. She couldn't fathom the situation she found herself in.

"Can I talk to her, at least?" Reva dropped her arms to her side, yielding completely. "I want to see where her head's at right now and what caused her to confess. She's not fooling me. I *know* she didn't do anything."

"I'll see what I can do. We can't allow her visitors right now, but you can check back later. I'll do everything I can to make sure you can talk to her."

Pistol purposely knocked over the detective's pen holder, causing a mess on the office floor. The detective huffed.

"I don't think your pet likes me much."

"I'd eat you if I could," Pistol replied as Reva picked him up in her hand.

As Matt leaned over to pick up his pens, she stared hard at his open laptop. Narrowing her eyes, she whispered a spell that discreetly shot a flurry of electrical energy straight out of her index finger and towards the laptop. Effectively frying the device, she watched in muted amusement as a puff of white smoke rose from the laptop and disappeared.

"Thank you for talking to me," she said, before exiting the office.

Matt straightened up, returned to his desk, and sat down, hoping to continue updating the case details. But his laptop didn't even turn on. The device showed a perpetual black screen that didn't budge no matter how forcefully he pressed onto the keyboard.

And an odd smell hung in the air. A sharp, acrid, burning smell.

"What?" Matt muttered. "This thing was working just fine a few minutes ago."

He continued trying to fix the issue himself, not knowing that the cause of his laptop's demise had walked out of the police station moments prior.

Chapter 30

"Thanks for visiting the Dimidio Inn. I hope you had a pleasant stay." Reva smiled at the couple on the other side of the front desk as she reached for their keys.

"It was great," the woman said. "You've done a wonderful job with this place."

"Thanks," Reva said. "We try to keep things authentic."

"I loved the little stories about the antique artwork," the woman gushed. "Did you make those up yourself?"

"Oh no," Reva said. "They came with the pictures."

"They're so detailed," the woman said. "It's like you really knew those artists."

"I wish," Reva tried to say smoothly. In reality, she did know the artists. She tried to keep mementos of various ghosts who had frequented the inn. But the mortals didn't need to know that.

With another quick check in her guest book, she put the finishing touches on the couple's bill.

"There was one thing," the man spoke for the first time.

"Yes?" Reva asked.

His partner looked worried. She grabbed the man's sleeve then let go.

"When we woke up this morning, there was this crack in our wall," he said.

Reva frowned.

"It wasn't there when we first got here," the woman broke in anxiously. "We made sure and a crack like that, we wouldn't have missed it."

"How big is it?" Reva asked.

The man held his hands apart to indicate a crack the size of a skateboard. Reva's frown deepened.

"And we couldn't have caused it," the woman said quickly. "I don't know what would have done something like that."

"Maybe foundational damage," the man suggested.

Reva doubted it. There was a lot more than architecture holding the building together.

"And you were in room seven?" she asked.

The couple nodded.

That had always been a room set aside for mortal visitors. There shouldn't have been anything supernatural tampering with that space. Unless it was tampering with the hotel in general.

"Well." Reve refocused on the concerned couple still staring at her. "It's an old building, what are you going to do?

"Thank you for bringing that to my attention. You won't be charged for any damages, of course. And I'll get that checked out as soon as possible."

"Oh, great."

They both sagged in relief. Reva turned back to her papers to hide a smile.

As the couple settled their bill, they promised to stay in touch and to come back to the Dimidio when they were in town for a wedding in the spring. They both waved and the woman held the door open for someone else just entering the lobby. Reva saw who was and immediately wanted to go back to bed.

Donna Corona pulled a brand-new pair of large sunglasses away from her face and smirked at Reva.

"Good morning," she said with a huge, toothy smile.

"Hi," Reva said.

"You don't sound very happy to see me," Donna said with a fake frown. She was even more smug than usual, glancing around the lobby like she couldn't wait to change it.

203

"Can't imagine why," Reva muttered under her breath.

"How's business?" Donna asked, ignoring Reva completely.

"Great," Reva said. "We're full for the next month." Which was true, just not with guests that Donna could see.

"Funny, you always claim to be full, but your lobby's always empty," Donna said snidely.

"I guess they're off enjoying all the wonderful things our town has to offer," Reva shot back.

"Maybe." Donna examined her nails. "How's your aunt doing?"

Reva faltered.

"She's doing fine," she said briskly.

"That's good," Donna cooed. "I was worried she'd be frightened."

"No," Reva said, trying to sound normal. "She has the morning off, so she's probably back at home. Probably knitting."

"Really?" Donna jerked her head up with a triumphant smile, her green eyes glowing. "I heard she spent the night at the police station."

"They've had questions for her. There is a murder investigation going on, after all," Reva said.

"If you needed a clearer sign that this town was begging to be revitalized," Donna sighed. "Anyway, that's not what I heard. They've got their killer because your aunt turned herself in."

With a jolt of realization like the cha-ching of a cash register, Reva understood what had happened. Donna's smug, triumphant attitude, how she already knew the details of what had happened to Auntie Alva, and how she hadn't even asked about buying the inn yet. It all made sense.

"It was you," Reva whispered.

"Excuse me?" Donna smiled brightly.

"What did you say to my aunt?"

"Are you sure you're okay, Reva?" Donna asked. "You're not making any sense."

"Stop pretending to be so innocent," Reva said. "This is all your fault. You must have blackmailed my aunt into confessing to a murder she didn't do. What did you say to her?"

"Just because I happened to know about your aunt's tragic fate, doesn't mean I had anything to do with it. You know how news travels in this town," Donna said.

Reva had to clench her fists at her side to keep from doing something she'd regret later.

"And besides," Donna went on. "She confessed, so that must have been what happened."

"You and I both know my aunt isn't a killer."

"People can surprise you," Donna said.

Unable to take it anymore, Reva stepped out from behind the front desk. Donna didn't blink, but she did take a step back.

Just as she was about to launch into a tirade, Reva pictured her aunt, scared and alone in jail. If she picked a fight with Donna now, Reva would create a whole new load of trouble, which would be of no use to Alva. Suddenly, Reva was more tired than angry.

"Why did you have to go after my aunt?" she demanded. "She didn't have anything to do with this. We could have handled this face-to-face."

"Oh, Reva." Donna rolled her eyes. "Haven't you figured me out yet? I don't care about the rules, I just want what's mine. If you don't want to give it to me, then I guess I'll have to take drastic measures. If you don't like my methods, then I suggest you get out of my way." Donna's level of drama would be laughable if she wasn't serious.

"I've had enough of this," Reva said. "You'll never get the Dimidio Inn. Now get off my property."

"Why?" Donna asked. "It'll be my property soon."

"You have no idea what you're dealing with," Reva said.

"I can't wait to find out," Donna said sweetly.

206

Unable to stand another second in Donna's presence, Reva ducked out the front door. She leaned back against the wall, breathing hard. Donna still didn't have the deed for the building, but without her aunt's help, it would be hard to the run the Inn by herself.

She didn't know what she was going to do.

Not for the first time, she wished for a partner. Cyrus was a wonderful friend and great with the ghosts, but she wanted someone who could truly exist in the mortal world. Who had her back at all times. She had no idea where she'd find someone like that.

She glanced back through the window. It wasn't safe to leave Donna on her own in the lobby. She was probably already drawing up plans to have the whole building torn down. Reva needed something to get rid of her and buy some time.

The answer came to her almost immediately.

She summoned her energy and stared hard at Donna's baby blue convertible. It was a beautiful machine.

Perfect.

Reva whispered a series of spells and the car shifted out of park. It sat still for a moment, then gravity began to take over. The car gently drifted backwards like a leaf on a lazy stream and headed towards the road.

Reva waited until the car was too far away to catch up to on foot, then slipped back into the lobby.

"Hey Donna?" she called.

Donna whirled around from where she was snooping into the guest book.

"Why didn't you leave your car in park?" Reva asked, gesturing over her shoulder.

Donna made a noise like a puppy falling off a table. She clutched her giant purse and lurched past Reva. As soon as she shouldered open the door, she let out a miserable wail.

Looking over Donna's shoulder, Reva could see that the car had made good progress. It had picked up speed in its trip across the parking lot and was about to sail across the road.

"Why does this always happen to me when I'm here?" Donna whimpered.

"No idea," Reva said.

The car flew across the road, jounced over the shoulder, and came to a shuddering stop in a ditch.

Chapter 31

After the commotion with Donna, Reva felt as though she desperately needed a change of scenery. She had hoped that giving Donna's precious car a few dings in a non-violent accident would make her feel better, but not even that could ease the pain of the current situation.

She felt as though she needed a change of scenery. She knew that everyone would be too busy gossiping about Alva to pay attention to what was happening in the inn, so she could take a bit of time to herself.

Reva sat down in the Yews Cemetery to think. The sun was beginning to move west in the sky, and she used the growing shadows being cast by the sun's rays to find a cool place to sit.

She couldn't decide if she wanted to think more about what poor Auntie Alva was going through or if she wanted to get her mind off of it. She desperately wanted to help her aunt but thinking about the current situation made her feel helpless and like her heart was being ripped in half.

She thought back to Donna and felt a surge of anger in her chest. Reva clenched her fist tightly. She couldn't believe how selfish that awful woman was. How dare she play with someone's life just so she could expand her business?

Cyrus saw Reva leave the inn and head towards the cemetery. He knew his friend would be in need of his comfort, so he wasn't too far behind.

He floated up next to Reva. He didn't need to be her closest friend to see how much she was hurting. The anger and pain and all of the other emotions she was feeling was written clearly across her face.

Cyrus sat down next to her in a patch of sunlight. The warmth didn't affect his ghostly form like it did her corporeal one.

"Is there anything I can do to help?" Cyrus's heart ached as he looked at her. Though he was usually able to grasp words with ease, he was having trouble finding the right things to say in this moment.

Reva sighed heavily.

"I just don't know what to do. I feel like I'm drowning."

"You are the master of your fate and the captain of your soul, my dear Reva. It may feel like you're drowning now, but this too shall pass."

"I just don't know if I believe that. Things have never looked this dire. Not ever."

"Things may look dire now, but they will get better. I can make sure of it."

"I can't ask you to take care of everything. This is my responsibility. Besides, it's a problem in the *mortal* world, not the supernatural one."

Cyrus hesitated for a moment. He knew he would move mountains for her if it meant he could see her smile. But he didn't want to admit that to her just yet. He needed to be a friend to her.

"I'll help in any way I can. I care about you very deeply."

"I know you do, Cyrus. Thank you. I don't know what I'd do without a friend like you."

He smiled gently at her.

"I'm happy I can be of some help at least. If standing by your side helps, then I am happy to do it."

"I just wish there was something I could do about Auntie Alva. She's being blackmailed by Donna. I just know it."

"Is there any way to prove that?"

"I don't think so. If she was arrested and confessed, short of finding the real murderer and irrefutable proof that Alva is innocent, I don't think the police will believe me when I tell them to trust me."

"I'm sure that bull-headed detective won't be of any help."

"No. Not at all. Not for this anyway. I wish there was some way I could solve the case."

"If it's something you want to do, I'm sure you can accomplish it. Your love for your aunt will carry you through this."

"I sure hope so." Reva looked like she didn't believe it.

She stood up suddenly. Sitting around had ceased to soothe her nerves. She looked around for something to do. She wanted to take action, but she didn't know how.

"Where are you going?" Cyrus asked.

"I don't know. I just have to do something. Anything."

She walked across the Yews. The place felt so familiar, but at the moment, that failed to bring her any comfort. She took long strides, heading towards the spot where Burton's body was found.

She stopped once she reached the area. Cyrus saw her eyes scanning the ground in front of her as if she was willing a clue to appear. The area had been searched several times already.

Cyrus looked as well. "Do you see anything interesting? Anything the police could have missed?"

"I don't think so," Reva said, shaking her head. She ran her hands over the seam of her jacket pockets, needing something to fiddle with as she looked. Her anger and frustration was making her feel antsy.

As Cyrus floated through the area, meticulously looking for any sort of strange disturbance that could have been missed, Reva shoved her hands in her jacket pockets. There, she found something she had forgotten about.

She ran her fingers over the object as she looked through the area with Cyrus. Her fingers stroked and fiddled with the bracelet given to her by Brenda. It was made by Natalie Owens, and Reva had thrown it in her pocket, forgetting about it until that moment.

Now it was the perfect object to play with while she was on edge.

She sighed. "I don't see anything."

"I don't either. I'm sorry, Reva."

"How did this all go so wrong, Cyrus?"

"Chin up, Reva. Let's get your mind off of this for now. Why don't I make us a little picnic?"

"A picnic?" The idea seemed absurd for a moment. How could they have a picnic while Alva was arrested? However, Reva had to admit to herself that the idea was tempting.

"Yes, a picnic. We'll sit out in the grass and enjoy the fresh air. It will be wonderful. And, as soon as we're done, we can focus on our next move. It won't do you much good to try to make a plan on an empty stomach."

Reva gave her friend a small smile. She was touched by the gesture. Though her heart still ached for Alva, she felt some solace in the comfort of her friendship.

213

"Alright. Let's go in and get the picnic basket."

"No, no. I'll go gather the things for the picnic. You just find a beautiful area where we can enjoy nature." Cyrus insisted.

Reva smiled at him. "You're too good to me, Cyrus."

"I hope that is true." Cyrus went off towards the inn in search of a picnic basket, food, and a blanket for them. Reva wandered through the Yews, wrapping her jacket around herself.

She found a nice warm and flat spot in the cemetery. She laid down on her back and closed her eyes, basking in the warm light of the sun. She ran her hands up and down the grass, feeling the long blades on her fingers and the palm of her hand.

She suddenly remembered the bracelet. She took it out of her pocket and twirled it between her fingers, examining it.

Some of the threads on the bracelet were coming loose. It was clearly a handmade bracelet. Though it was nice, it didn't have the structural integrity of something made by a factory.

As she was looking at the bracelet, Reva heard a long, low whistle. She sat up, looking for the source of the noise.

Her eyes scanned the tree line, and she saw a ghost girl in her late teens. Reva recognized her as Faye Young. She stood underneath a tree, looking at Reva.

"Excuse me, miss. Where did you get that bracelet?" She called out.

Chapter 32

Reva looked at Faye, wondering why the ghost was asking her about the bracelet she held in her hands. It wasn't anything special. Dozens of them, if not more, surely, were made.

"Someone gave it to me." Reva called back, still unsure of the ghost's intentions.

Faye moved a bit closer to Reva. She came more into view as she walked. Without the large tree making her seem smaller, she appeared more adult than she had before. Reva didn't feel as though she was in danger, but she was terribly confused about the situation. Why would a ghost be interested in such a thing?

Faye crossed over the graves in the cemetery. She had a small smile on her face and seemed to be enjoying her stroll. She kept looking at the bracelet. Reva wondered if perhaps she was lonely and wanted to talk.

"Really? What a wonderful gift. It's so pretty."

Reva regarded the bracelet again. Parts of the phone wire were coming loose. She felt a tingle in the back of her brain. She felt as though she was reminded of something, but she wasn't sure what.

Something about the bracelet had seemed familiar, though she wasn't able to put her finger on the answer. She looked at its shape and the feeling of the wire, unable to get a handle on her initial recognition.

"Yes, I suppose it's nice," Reva said.

"Oh yes, it's so interesting. I see many bracelets with jewels and such, but this is more unique I think."

"I guess so. What do you like about it?"

"Oh, well I think it's such a lovely color," Faye said, floating over to her, regarding the bracelet. She smiled at Reva as she did.

There was a flash of memory in Reva's mind. She had seen this color before. She searched her memory, trying to figure out why it suddenly seemed familiar.

The color was important. She had seen something this color and even the shape before. She just couldn't figure out where.

"It is a lovely color, isn't it?" Reva said, her voice trailing off at the end.

She focused in on the bracelet, trying to examine every inch of it and insert it into every part of the investigation she had catalogued into her mind. There was something there. She just knew it.

"I think I've seen this before." She said out loud, but mostly to herself.

"Well yes, it's your bracelet. I'm sure you saw it when it was given to you." Faye said with a laugh.

"No, I mean somewhere else... Maybe it was a different one..."

Faye said something else, but Reva was too focused on the bracelet to hear. It was as though she was entranced by it. Where had she seen it before?

An anxious part of her wondered if she had seen Alva with the bracelet, though the rational part of her mind knew that wasn't the case. It wasn't something Alva would wear.

Finally, after so much frustration, there was a clue. She couldn't understand why that information was so hard to recall. It was as though her mind all lit up at once.

"Oh, I didn't realize you'd appreciate the compliment so much," Faye said, reacting to Reva's visible change in demeanor.

"No, sorry. I just remembered something."

Reva thought back to the things the police collected from the crime scene. She was sure her faint, tickling memory emanated from there. The moment in time was hazy in her memory. So much had happened all at once.

217

However, she knew now where she had seen the bracelet, or at least something that exact color. For the first time since Alva's arrest, Reva felt hopeful.

Cyrus walked over to Reva, picnic basket in hand. He saw her sitting in the grass regarding something in her hand. Faye Young was nearby peering at the object as well.

"Ah, hello," he said. He had filled the basket with Reva's favorite treats from the kitchen. He thought she deserved something special after the day she had.

But then he saw a thought pass through Reva's mind. He didn't need to be her best friend to realize she had stumbled across something important. Her eyes went from glazed over to bright and lit up. She suddenly jumped up from her seated position. The look of anger and depression she wore before had completely left her face.

"What's happened? Have you figured something out?" Cyrus asked. He regarded Reva curiously. He had only been gone a few minutes, but somehow quite a bit had changed in his absence.

"I have an idea, Cyrus." Reva was practically bouncing on her heels with excitement.

"An idea? What sort of idea?"

"I don't know yet. I just thought of something that may help us."

Reva started marching with purpose towards the cemetery exit. Faye gave her a little wave as she headed back towards the tree line. Cyrus looked between the two of them, confused. He wondered what he had missed while preparing the picnic.

"Reva, wait. What about our picnic?" Cyrus chased after her as she went.

Reva stopped and turned around. She looked apologetic. "Oh, I'm so sorry, Cyrus. I got so swept up in everything. Would we be able to take a raincheck?"

Cyrus tried to not let his disappointment show. Though it was just a simple picnic between friends, he always cherished every moment he was with Reva. However, he knew that whatever she realized must be something urgent.

"Of course. It seems like this is terribly important. This is what you were waiting for, right?"

Reva nodded. She felt the butterfly wings flapping in her stomach. If her hunch was right, she would be able to blow this case wide open and free Alva.

"I can tell how important this is, Reva. Please, don't stop your investigation on my account." He gave her a smile, which she returned. He began to head back towards the inn, but Reva called out to him.

"Wait, Cyrus! Where are you going?" Cyrus stopped and turned towards her, surprised.

"I was just going to put everything away. Then I supposed I planned to watch the front desk. Why do you ask?"

Reva chuckled. Cyrus was always so funny about things like this. She knew that she needed help, and what better way to continue her investigation than with her best friend by her side? "Well, you're coming with me, of course."

"Oh, my apologies. I didn't realize that was the case." Cyrus tried not to smile as he felt his heart, which had stopped beating so long ago, flutter.

"Here, I'll help you put everything away. Then we'll put a sign on the door saying we'll be back soon."

She walked towards the inn with him. She kept a quick pace. She wanted to make their next move quickly.

"Where do you plan to go?" he asked.

"The local high school."

Cyrus was surprised by her answer. He couldn't imagine what could be so important at the high school. "Really? What's there?"

"I just have a hunch that it will lead us to the information we're looking for."

Cyrus still wasn't sure what exactly she meant, but he nodded, agreeing to help her continue.

Reva and Cyrus entered the inn. He put away the blanket while she quickly unpacked the picnic basket so none of the food would go bad. She smiled as she realized he had picked out her favorite things. She thought to herself how wonderful it was to have a friend who cared so much.

Cyrus reentered the room as Reva put the basket away.

"Well, are you ready?" He asked.

"Yes. I am." Reva responded. She had a look of determination that Cyrus recognized, but never before had the stakes been so high.

"I am pleased you're not feeling so overwhelmed anymore," he said to her as they headed for the door.

"I feel like I can do something now. That's really what I needed."

"Then I'm happy it happened."

Cyrus followed her out of the inn and into her car. He was still unsure what they were going to the high school for or how it would help, but as he watched Reva steer away from the inn with determination, he knew he would follow her anywhere.

Chapter 33

"I still don't think we should be here," Cyrus moaned.

Reva pulled her car into an open space in the parking lot of the bakery across from the high school.

"I thought we were going to the high school?"

"We are," Reva said. "But you're right, we shouldn't be there. If anyone sees the car, they can think I was buying a croissant."

"You wouldn't just buy a croissant," Cyrus said. "It would be a chocolate croissant."

"Good point," Reva agreed. A chocolate croissant sounded amazing.

"Great," Cyrus said happily. "Let's go."

"Not so fast," Reva groaned. "We're on a mission. Pastries later." She hopped out of the car and hurried across the parking lot.

"You're no fun," Cyrus grumbled as he hurried to keep up with her.

"Neither is jail," Reva muttered.

She waited for a truck to cross in front of her then darted across the street. At the outskirts of the school grounds, she stayed close to the line of trees near the giant sign that read, "Shadow Woods High" in large red and white letters.

From her own time at this school, she had plenty of experience wandering around the campus unnoticed. But there had been some updates since she was a student.

"Help me find any security cameras, okay?"

"Got it," Cyrus said. As a ghost, he had a particularly sensitive relationship to electricity that would probably come in handy.

222

They trooped around the science building to where the track looped around the football field. Half of the track was bathed in shadow from the looming mouth of the bleachers. The track team was out for practice, clumps of runners going at different speeds and several people waiting their turn for the long jump.

The whole field was bordered by a tall chain-link fence. Reva knew that climbing it would be impossible.

"Did you do school sports?" Cyrus asked.

"Everybody did," Reva said. "But I wasn't very good at it."

"Don't be so hard on yourself. What was your favorite?"

"I don't know," Reva said thoughtless. "Volleyball?" She scanned for the coaches and found them deep in conversation near the starting line. "Did they even have school sports when you were alive?" she asked.

"Of course," Cyrus said. "When I was a boy, I played tennis and rugby."

Reva blinked, totally distracted. She stared at Cyrus's delicate frame. "You played rugby?"

"I didn't say that I excelled," Cyrus said. "I said that I participated."

"That sounds more like it." She took one more look at the coaches. "Okay, let's go."

223

She strode purposefully and quickly around the edge of the playing field, trying to make it look like she was supposed to be there.

"What are we looking for?" Cyrus asked.

"There used to be a gap in the fence where we'd sneak out after practice, but this is a new fence," Reva said. "We need to find a way in."

"Here." Cyrus easily slipped through and stood on the other side of the fence.

"Great for you," Reva teased. "What about me?"

"Can't you use magic to blast your way through?" Cyrus asked.

Reva tested the fence. It had probably been put up in the past few years. The structure was still solid. She'd be exhausted from the effort of trying to "magic" her way through.

"Not if I don't want everyone to know we're here," she said. "Come on."

They set off again. Reva ducked behind bushes or cars whenever they got too close to the track. No one seemed to notice the strange woman on the other side of the fence.

By the time they reached the bleachers, the sun had sunk low enough that the shadows stretched to the doors to the locker rooms. Reva paused just out of sight.

"Well? See any security cameras?"

Cyrus looked ahead.

"Two," he said. "One by those giant steps and one next to that grate that says 'Concessions'."

"Great." Reva nodded her thanks. She summoned up her energy, whispered a quick series of spells, and sent a burst of electrical magic to fry both cameras. Even from her hiding place, she could see the halo of blue sparks that sprang from each unit.

"I must say, you are getting quite good at that," Cyrus said.

"Thanks," Reva said. "Now there must be a gate around here somewhere."

Sure enough, once they reached the backside of the bleachers, there was a tall gate held closed by a padlock.

"Piece of cake," she said. With a quick jerk of her magic, the lock crumpled and snapped apart. The pieces landed on the concrete with a dull clatter.

"You're a little scary, you know that?" Cyrus said.

"Is that a compliment?" Reva asked as she pushed the gate open just enough to slide through.

"Oh yes," Cyrus said, hurrying after her.

Standing under the bleachers brought back memories of football games with her friends and family. In the eerie, afternoon quiet, she felt like a just as much of a ghost as Cyrus.

225

"By the way, do you even know what you're looking for?" he asked.

Reva did. "It's going to be a door marked 'Equipment' or something like that," she said.

"I only see doors marked 'Bathroom'," Cyrus said.

By the time they reached the other side of the bleachers, Reva had fried three more security cameras, but there was no sign of anything useful.

"Well," Cyrus said sadly. "I guess that's it, we'll have to give up." He began to turn back the way they had come.

"And give up on Auntie Alva?" Reva said. "I'm going to tell her you said that."

"You wouldn't dare!" Cyrus caught up with her on the other side of the bleachers.

While they had been out of sight, the track team had finished their practice and the field was empty. That was when Reva saw the nondescript white shed by the far end zone.

"Bingo," she said.

When they reached the shed, the door was held shut with another heavy lock. Reva quickly destroyed it, barely feeling the exertion of her magic through the adrenaline coursing through her veins. Inside was a jumbled heap of sporting equipment.

226

"I'm confused," Cyrus said, peering over Reva's shoulder.

"Look, maybe I'm wrong." Reva began to sort through the contents of the shed. "But I think the answer to our problems is in this shed."

She kicked kickballs, tossed footballs, threw baseballs and basketballs, and held her nose at handfuls of stinky uniforms. Just as she was untangling herself from a giant net, she saw something long and pointy sticking out from under a pile of hockey sticks.

"There!" She lurched forward and pulled out a hunter's bow.

"Oh my," Cyrus said. "I didn't know they had an archery team at this school."

Reva's hands shook as she examined the bow. Even though it had been hidden in the back of the shed, it was clearly in good condition and had been used recently.

"We need to take this to Matt Carver right away," she said.

"We do?" He took a step back as Reva struggled out of the shed and pulled the door closed.

"I don't see why I have to get involved," Cyrus called, trailing after Reva as she hurried back across the field.

"You're already involved," Reva retorted.

"Excuse me, I've only been a supporting player."

227

"Cyrus." Reva took a deep breath to summon her patience. It felt like time was slipping through her fingers. "This could be the key to keeping Auntie Alva out of prison for good."

"But why Carver?" Cyrus crossed his arms over his chest. "Hasn't that fellow already proven untrustworthy many times over?"

"I know, I know," Reva said. "But this time we don't have a choice. He's the only one that can help."

"Can't we just tell him the bow is here?" Cyrus asked. "You don't have to risk getting caught with it, imagine how that would look."

It would look bad, Reva conceded. "Someone could get to it first," she said. "It has to be now, and it has to be me."

Cyrus stared at her and Reva remembered that he was only trying to look out for her.

"Please?" she asked. "I can't lose my aunt."

"Okay." Cyrus nodded. "Let's go."

He hurried next to her as they left the playing field. In her haste to get back to the car, she was less careful than she should have been. Twice, Cyrus had to warn her about teachers heading to their cars or parents picking up their kids.

"What would I do without you?" she said gratefully.

"Luckily, you'll never have to find out."

Chapter 34

With a duffle bag from her trunk over her shoulder, Reva made her way into the Shadow Woods Police Department. Standing in front of the receptionist's desk, she waited until Miriam finished her phone call before turning her attention to Reva.

"Hello again, ma'am. I assume you want to speak with Detective Matt Carver again, correct?"

"You know me so well," Reva replied, readjusting her hold on the bag. In one of her fists, she held the bracelet made out of phone wires. "I hope he's not busy right now."

"He isn't, ma'am. He just finished a meeting with another officer, and doesn't have another one scheduled for the rest of the day. You can go ahead."

Nodding, Reva hurried to his office. As usual for her, she didn't knock before entering his office. She just opened the door and hoped that he didn't respond too negatively to her presence.

Matt read a newspaper on his desk, sipping a hot cup of coffee as he did so. He looked up from his paper, eyeing Reva and the duffle bag with immediate concern. Reva Brennan was an enigma to him, one that he was still trying to figure out.

"What do you have in that bag?"

"The clue that may help tie this investigation together."

"What are you–"

She dropped the duffle bag on his desk, knocking over a few things with the brusque action. Matt rolled his eyes, glaring up at her for nearly spilling the coffee mug on the brand new laptop that he just received from his superiors. He secured a mild scolding for somehow destroying the computer.

"You said you wanted to find the murder weapon, right?"

"Yes, but…" Matt's eyes widened. "You didn't."

After tossing him the bracelet in her hand, she crossed her arms over her chest. She waited for him to inspect the evidence with a stone-faced expression.

He sent her a dubious look before standing up and opening the duffle bag. Inside, a large hunting bow.

"Reva, how did you find this?" Matt's words sounded airy, in pure disbelief. Reva didn't think she had ever heard him like that before. "Don't get me wrong, I'm impressed, but I just don't understand how you managed this."

"I knew that my aunt wasn't the one who killed Burton. I tried telling you this, but–"

"I need you to realize that I had a lot of evidence and details to look over. I didn't know whether to trust you or not because of the conversation we had before. I'm sorry, Reva, but I thought you were lying just to cover up for your aunt."

"Well." Reva gestured to the bow and the bracelet. "I hope you can now realize that I'm a person of my word. I wouldn't lie about something as serious as this. I love my aunt, but if she was *truly* responsible for killing that man, I wouldn't have gone through the lengths I did to protect her."

"Do you mean that?" Matt raised a brow. "That's easy to say when you've never been in a situation like that before. People can do questionable things to protect the people they love."

"I mean it, Matt."

His mouth opened slightly, as if ready to respond. However, he closed it soon afterwards. His dark eyes twinkled with rapt curiosity, with the main culprit of his fascination standing right in front of him.

"So where did you find this weapon?" Matt asked. "I had all of my officers scouring throughout town for it. We've looked in dumpsters, trash cans… I even made a few of them stop by the town dump to see if they could find anything useful. I don't think they like me that much after making them do that."

"I can understand," she quipped. "You made them go through a lot when, in reality, the bow was closer than you think."

231

"We were having a good moment and you're starting to act sarcastic again."

"I'm not!" Reva countered. "I just want you to realize how much of an asset I was in this investigation, and if you would have let me help from the start–"

"You know I couldn't just do that. You're a civilian."

"This civilian just helped you crack this case, all while making sure you didn't jail an innocent for a crime she didn't commit," she replied. "That would have been a blow to your reputation, I'm sure."

Pressing his lips into a thin line, Matt didn't respond to that statement. He gazed at the bow.

"And you're sure this is the murder weapon we're looking for?"

"I think so, yes. I'm not an expert at these things, but it looks strong enough to send an arrow through someone's chest." Shrugging, Reva thought back on Sybil. "At the very least, this might be the bow that was stolen from a local hunter also connected to the investigation. Sybil Zimmerman."

Matt exhaled softly, shaking his head.

"It's amazing how you managed to dig up all this information on your own," he admitted. "People are incredibly capable whenever they're motivated by something they care about."

"I agree. My aunt was the driving force behind everything," she replied. "Talking to Sybil Zimmerman and Brenda Braceling led me to this point."

"Brenda, too?" Matt asked. "When I talked to her, she led me towards Mackie Crabb, but he wasn't involved in this murder. He hit his brother in front of multiple witnesses, sure, but he wasn't at *The Yews* when Burton was killed. I doubt the guy could even shoot a bow and arrow with how drunk he was."

"She was well-intentioned, but a little misguided." Reva reached over, pointing to the bracelet she dropped on his desk. "That's our clue, Matt. This bracelet right here."

Gazing down at the small accessory, his eyes widened once a realization hit him dead-on. He then searched through his cabinet files, hastily sifting through the multiple labelled folders until he found the one he needed. Setting it upon his desk, he opened it and started looking through the photographs the crime scene investigators took of the scene.

He glanced at Reva from underneath his brows. "Where did you get this from?"

"I just told you. Brenda Braceling gave it to me."

"That's..." Matt stopped flipping through the documents once he found a particular photograph that he held up closer to his eyes. "That bracelet..."

"I know," she said.

"How?" His eyes narrowed. "I didn't think this information was made available to the public. At least, not to my knowledge."

"Well, I heard some people talking about it in town. An officer said that they found a piece of yellow phone wire near the body, but they didn't think much of it because they assumed it wasn't part of the case."

Lying on the spot like that made her heart skip a beat. At least, she didn't have to admit that a young spirit in a graveyard led her down the right path. Matt probably would kick her out of his office for a statement like that. She kept assuming that a mortal as astute as he was wouldn't take too well to the idea of spirits and the afterlife. She didn't plan to test that hypothesis.

"Huh…" Matt clicked his tongue in thought. "Did you find out which officer was talking so openly about the case? I think that's a security breach of some sort."

"No, sorry," she replied, hoping that he didn't catch on. "I heard about this information indirectly, so I didn't see who the officer was, unfortunately."

"I see." He handed over the photograph. "Take a look."

A few feet away from Burton's body, the crime scene photographers took images of a small piece of yellow phone wire nearby.

"In my notes, we decided that the phone wire wasn't going to make that much of a difference, but it's good practice to write down everything we find even if we think it's just litter."

"Obviously, it did." Reva nodded towards the bracelet again as she returned the photograph back into the folder. "There's only one person I know of who was making these bracelets. Not only that, but she had a vendetta against Burton for spreading lies about her deceased ancestors with his ghost tours. It's clear as day."

"Reva, how did you manage to figure this out by yourself?"

"I told you already. I wasn't going to rest until I cleared my aunt's name from this investigation. It took its toll, for sure. I think I have permanent bags under my eyes now, but it's all worth it." She sent him a genuine smile, the first of many more. "I found out who killed Burton."

Chapter 35

The next morning, crowds of citizens and reporters gathered in front of the Shadow Woods Police Department. Chief of Police Lucas Murray called for a press conference to inform the town about the latest developments regarding Burton Crabb's murder case.

When Reva arrived, she found it difficult to maneuver her car through the masses. She moved slowly, eventually finding a spot close to the main event. Her motive wasn't to stick around, however.

Aunt Alva waited for her outside the police station. She sat on a bench bordering the building's front wall, watching from afar as the press conference took place in the station's parking lot. Reva caught a glimpse of Matt, standing beside his superior as the Chief of Police addressed the anticipating crowd. Taking a seat beside her aunt, she sighed.

"I'm glad you're alright," she said, placing a hand on her aunt's knee. "I still don't understand why you did that."

"The threat seemed credible, my dear."

"From who?"

The concerned glaze that passed over Auntie Alva's eyes, as well as her hesitance to admit who it was, said it all for Reva.

"I knew it."

"Don't do anything silly. It's done and over with."

"Donna Corona isn't going to leave us alone until I sell her that hotel," she said brusquely. "I'm never going to sell her *The Dimidio Inn*, so she's going to continue these intimidation tactics until I give in. *You* cannot cave into her demands, Auntie, no matter how credible they seem."

236

"She said if I didn't take the blame, she would find another way to hurt you. I couldn't bear the thought, my dear. I couldn't."

"How would she hurt me, Auntie? One snap of my finger and I can break both of her kneecaps."

"Please, don't. You know how I feel about the unnecessary use of violence."

Sighing, Reva leaned until her back hit the building. The conference continued on as they chatted, with Matt already taking the podium from the Chief of Police to explain that they finally found the individual responsible for Burton Crabb's murder. Natalie Owens, local softball coach for Shadow Woods High.

"You helped him figure this case out, didn't you?"

Reva nodded. "They arrested her late last night. Natalie hated Burton Crabb for the lies he perpetrated about her ancestors. She caught him, alone and vulnerable in the middle of *The Yews* that night, piercing an arrow straight through his heart with the bow she stole from Sybil Zimmerman," she explained. Matt gave the same amount of details to the crowd, who snapped photos and videos with their phones. "She didn't anticipate leaving behind a small piece of phone wire, which helped me connect things back to her."

"Why did you go through so much?" Aunt Alva asked genuinely, tucking a hair strand behind Reva's ear.

"You didn't have to. I'm sure Detective Carver would have figured things out eventually."

"I'm sure." Reva rolled her eyes. "He would have spent too long investigating and you would have been left behind in a jail cell for a crime you didn't commit. That sounds like a great alternative."

"So, you took the reins yourself?"

"Of course, I did. I pieced everything together. Brenda Braceling gave me the bracelet, which flipped the investigation on its head. I didn't even consider Natalie Owens as a suspect, but I remembered how passionately she spoke about righting the wrongs Burton inflicted on her family's name. It didn't hit me until recently. Finding Sybil's stolen bow in her belongings at the high school was the nail in the coffin."

"You have a knack for this, my dear. Perhaps, you should ask Detective Carver if you can work for him sometime."

"That's never going to happen, Auntie," she replied, nearly dry heaving at the thought. "Limiting my contact with him from now on is the main reason why I'm glad this investigation is over. That, and clearing your name."

"I can't believe how adamantly you dislike that poor young man," Auntie Alva said in astonishment, taking a glimpse at the detective as he addressed the eager swarm of

238

reporters that stuck their microphones in his face. "He did a good job."

"Thanks to me," she deadpanned. "I told him he could take all the credit if he wanted to. The only thing I asked for in return was your expedited release from jail. I'm glad he went through with his side of the deal."

"Me too, my dear. Staying in a jail cell isn't my preferred environment. It's far too cold and dingy for my liking."

"I'm sorry you went through that, Auntie." Reva wrapped her arm around her aunt, pulling her head onto her shoulder. "I won't let it happen again. And when I see Donna Corona again—"

"You won't do anything," Aunt Alva interjected sternly, sending her a pointed look. "The woman is a nuisance, I understand, but that doesn't mean you need to jeopardize your reputation just to get a hand over her. It's not wise."

"She wants our hotel," Reva lamented, rubbing circles into her aunt's shoulder. "She's ruthless about it. First, she hired a child to throw rocks through the window. Now, she blackmailed you to confess to a murder that you had no part in. What's next, Auntie? Should I just lay down and take the next scheme of hers without putting up a fight?"

"No, of course not. You need to handle individuals like Donna Corona carefully. Attacking them outright isn't the smart thing to do."

"Well, I don't know how else to deal with her, so let's just hope I don't catch her alone in an alleyway somewhere."

Tuning back into the conference, she heard one of the reporters ask how Matt managed to solve the case. His eyes flitted over towards hers and he smiled briefly before answering the reporter's question, who hastily wrote the answer down in his notes to use as an attractive headline later.

"I presume that you and the detective are going to get along eventually."

"C'mon, Auntie, don't say things like that."

"You keep denying it, but there's going to come a day where you'll enjoy his company," Aunt Alva said, bumping shoulders with her niece. "Just saying. When have I been wrong about these things?"

"You sound pretty wrong right now."

"Does he know about your magic yet?"

"Auntie!" Reva knitted her eyebrows together, appalled by the mere suggestion. "He's never going to know about that!"

"Why not? If you continue solving cases with him, I'm sure the conversation will arise in time whether you want it to or not. You can't hide such an integral part of your life forever."

Reva scoffed. "You act as if he's going to be some huge piece of my life moving forward. He's not. He's just the newbie detective who caught a break because I managed to help him with his first murder case." Standing up from the bench, Reva offered a hand to her aunt. "Let's go. I don't want to watch this conference anymore. It's making me regret letting him take all the credit."

"Jealous of his spotlight, I see?"

She glanced in his direction, seeing him practically glow with the limelight and praise. In the back of her mind, she figured staying out of police business was the right choice. However, she wondered, just for a moment, what it would feel like to stand on that podium and take the credit for solving such an important case to the town.

She would never know.

"Not at all," she answered, leading the way to her car. "I need to talk to you about something else, anyway. It's important."

"More so than the culmination of this murder case? I kind of wanted to see the end."

"I'm sure all the town's newspapers will give a detailed commentary on what happened here later. Come in."

Reva opened the passenger door for her Auntie. Once inside, she hurried over to the driver's seat.

"What's happening now, my dear? I don't like that look on your face."

"Auntie, I don't know where to begin. I've had a strange feeling for a while, but I thought it was just in my head. Recently, Cyrus and Pistol started bringing things to my attention and I can't ignore this sensation anymore. Something bad might happen if I do."

"Honey, what are you talking about?" Auntie Alva pressed the back of her hand on Reva's forehead. "You aren't catching a fever, aren't you? You tend to ramble nonsensically when you do."

"No, Auntie! I'm serious about this. It keeps bothering me and it might affect my business if we sit around and do nothing."

"What?" Aunt Alva asked, desperately waiting for a clear answer.

Reva let out a tremulous sigh.

"Auntie Alva... Something isn't right with the hotel."

Thank you for reading!

Printed in Great Britain
by Amazon